Seizing Mack

A Contemporary Love Story

Covendale Series, Book 3

Abbie Zanders

This is a work of fiction. Similarities to real people, places, or
events are entirely coincidental.

Seizing Mack

First edition. October, 2018.

Copyright © 2018 Abbie Zanders.

Written by Abbie Zanders.

ISBN: 9781728796338

Acknowledgements

Amazing cover and series design by Marisa @ www.covermedarling.com

Stock photos from www.depositphotos.com and www.pixabay.com

Professional editing by Meg at mededits.com. Proofreading by Carol at Editing by Carol Tietsworth.

… and THANK YOU to all of *you* for selecting this book. You didn't have to, but you did.

Before You Begin

Seizing Mack is the third book in my Covendale series (the first is Five Minute Man; the second, All Night Woman).

The series embraces small town romance with lots of sarcasm, humor, and flawed, realistic, relatable characters.

Occasional strong language and sexy times make this a good choice for mature readers. However, if these things offend you, this probably isn't the book for you.

Still with me? Awesome.

If you like what you read, feel free to check out my other titles and click the link at the back of this book to sign up for my newsletter, receive a free ebook, and get a chance each month to win a $25 gift card, just for being your snarky, alpha-male loving self.

Chapter One

~ Nick ~

Nick Benning was finally *home*. A sense of familiarity settled around him, warm and comforting. Things really hadn't changed that much. Lots of mountains. Lots of farms. Lots of family owned businesses that had been around since long before he was born. Covendale was the same sleepy small town it had always been.

He was different, though.

When he'd left he'd been young, not just in body but in mind and spirit. Barely out of college, he'd believed the best part of his life was already over. The jury was still out on that, but after ten long years, he was finally ready to move forward. To do that, he had to face his past.

He cruised the main street, his memories tangling with his skills of trained observation, creating a weave of past and present. A few faces looked familiar, but not many would recognize him now. His shoulders were broader; his face, no longer smooth and unlined. The glossy black Charger he had now was nothing like the classic 1966 Shelby Mustang GT350 that had been his baby back then.

He drove past Kelner's Drugstore and made a right onto Tanner Avenue. A new shopping center had sprung up around Lou's, his favorite burger joint, but they'd managed to maintain the small-town feel. Kudos to the town planning commission for that.

He kept going, past the town proper, into the surrounding outskirts, where communities of single family homes provided a couple-mile wide buffer between the bustling downtown area and the patchwork expanse of farms and forest.

The house he'd grown up in was still there, a brown and white Tudor-style split level nestled between a brick rancher and a two-story colonial. The tree where he and his sister Liz had once swung on a tire swing was gone, the front yard too perfect and meticulously landscaped to believe any children lived there now.

His parents no longer lived there, choosing to forego the brutal northeast winters and spend their golden years in the Sunshine State instead. Liz was still in the area, though. Last he'd heard, she'd moved into a townhouse after their folks had moved to Florida. That didn't surprise him at all. Outdoor chores like mowing the lawn and raking the leaves had never appealed to her.

Liz was one of the primary reasons he'd chosen to return to his roots. He hadn't seen or spoken to her in years. She'd written him often at first, her correspondence filled with a combination of sympathy, hope, and general information he hadn't been able to process then, when the pain had been too fresh. He hadn't done a very good job of keeping in touch beyond a birthday card once a year or a change of address note when he thought about it.

He felt bad about that. Liz deserved better, but he also knew she understood. Losing his fiancée had gutted him. Going away was the only way he'd been able to go on at the time. If he'd stayed in Covendale, he might never have dug himself out of the pit of guilt, anger and grief that possessed him after Annie's tragic death.

He was older and wiser now; it was time to face his demons and put them to rest. Bad things happened. Not just to him, but to everyone at some point or another. The world kept turning, regardless. He'd grieved long enough and it was time to start living again. To start *feeling* again.

Reconnecting with Liz was an integral part of his plan, though he'd been unsuccessful at reaching her. He'd called several times over the past few weeks, leaving messages with his mobile number and a request to call him back.

So far, she hadn't.

That was disappointing, but not entirely unexpected. He hadn't exactly been the poster boy for callbacks and keeping in touch. To be fair, he hadn't told her *why* he was reaching out after being incommunicado for so long, either. He'd been hoping to lay some groundwork with a bit of catching up first before dropping the big stuff, like the fact that he was back not just for a visit, but staying for good.

Once he'd made the decision to return, however, things had fallen into place much quicker than he'd anticipated. The Covendale PD had recently created a new position for a dedicated drug enforcement operator that was right up his alley. His six-month transition suddenly became six weeks, and now here he was, pulling into her driveway unannounced and unexpected.

Would she envelop him in one of her strangling hugs or slam the door in his face? With Liz, he could see things going either way. She had the biggest heart of anyone he knew, but even she had her limits. His leaving she would understand. His lack of communication since, not so much.

Well, that was all about to change. He pressed the softly glowing doorbell, hearing a faint echo of chimes within. What he didn't hear was anyone approaching to answer the door. He waited a good minute before ringing again with the same result.

Liz didn't appear to be home.

Feeling a mixture of relief and disappointment, Nick got back into his car. His plan had been to give his sister a heads-up before she heard of his return from someone else; thinking that, with luck, their long overdue reunion would go well and they'd spend his first Sunday afternoon back in town catching up. But, he thought as he drove away, maybe having a few more days to reacclimate first was a good thing.

~ * ~

Bright and early Monday morning, Nick headed down to the police station to officially start his new job. The current Chief of Police, Sam Brown, seemed like a good guy, tough but fair. Sam hadn't been the CoP ten years ago when everything had gone down, but he had been on the force and was familiar with Nick's history. They'd spoken over the phone several times after Nick had expressed an interest in returning to his roots and Sam had been instrumental in making that happen.

He parked the Charger in the public lot behind the station, one of several that served local businesses and kept the on-street parking to a minimum. It was a good car, strong and powerful, but it wasn't his Shelby. After years in storage, it would probably take some tuning up to get it running smoothly again, but tinkering with his baby again was one of the things he was looking forward to most.

As he walked past the large sculpture commemorating local service men and women, he took a moment to appreciate the architecture of his new workplace. The Covendale Police Station had been built from blocks of local granite more than a hundred years earlier. It looked like it, too, with its stately columns and stone arches over tall, narrow windows.

The inside was far more modern. Unlike the big city stations he was used to, the ground floor lobby resembled a cozy waiting room. Behind a polished wooden counter, a pleasant-looking woman in her late forties offered a friendly smile.

"You must be Nick Benning," she said, rising from her seat.

"I am. What gave me away?"

"The suit." She laughed, her eyes twinkling. He liked her instantly. "Sam told me you were coming. It's all he's been talking about for weeks. He's already planning a welcome barbecue for you this weekend. I'm Gail Brown, by the way. Sam's wife."

Nick kept his smile light and friendly, though he wasn't sure how he felt about a 'welcome barbecue'. Being the center of attention had never been his thing. "It's a pleasure to meet you, Mrs. Brown."

"Gail, please. We're on a first name basis around here."

"Gail," he corrected.

"Good." Gail handed him a small flexible binder. "Here's all the legal stuff — employment contract, benefits, insurance info. Where are you staying?"

"The Twin Pines motel."

"Oh, the Twin Pines is nice! Won't do for long term, though. My sister is a realtor with a real gift for finding people their perfect space. I can give you her number."

For years he'd been living a transitory existence, moving from one city to another, and that had worked for him. Now that he'd come home, he wanted something more permanent, a place that he could call his own. That would take some time, though. He had specific ideas of what he wanted — something cozy yet spacious, earthy yet modern. In the meantime, he needed a place to live, and his requisites for temporary housing were more flexible.

"Does she do leases?"

"She does."

"Great. Thank you, Gail. I appreciate that."

She beamed. "You're very welcome. Now, go on up. Third floor. Sam's expecting you. Oh, and one more thing."

"Yes?"

"How do you like your coffee?"

"Coffee?"

"Yep. We've got a nice thing going with

Ground Zero. They deliver fresh at the beginning of every shift. You won't find better."

"Black. And strong."

"Typical." She laughed again. "Got it."

Nick bypassed the elevator, preferring to take the stairs to the third floor. As he mounted the steps, he couldn't help but be pleasantly surprised with his initial welcome. He'd feared it would be awkward; that each time someone looked at him it would be with curiosity, associating him with what had happened long ago, but so far, no one had given any indication that they either knew or cared.

He tempered those thoughts with cautious optimism. Small town folks had long memories. Gail was only the first person he'd talked to who might know something of his background. The real test would come in the ensuing days and weeks.

The top floor of the station was as nice as the ground floor. Natural light spilled in from big, open windows across cool, neutral tones. The carpet looked fairly new, as did the furnishings. Half of the space contained L-shaped, open workspaces, three of which were presently occupied. The other half held a conference room and the chief's office.

"Nick Benning."

Nick turned to face the guy closest to him, immediately creating a profile out of habit. Early thirties, like him, perhaps a few years younger. Athletic build, blonde hair, blue eyes. The ID badge he wore identified him as Detective Kent Emerson.

The guy held out his hand. "Welcome. The chief said you were coming in today."

Nick accepted his hand, returning Emerson's firm grip with one of his own. "So much for a quiet entrance."

Kent laughed, a little too loudly. "Forewarned is forearmed, as they say. Coming in from Chicago, huh? That's quite a change."

Unlike Gail, Kent's friendliness was less sincere and more calculating. Kent was sizing him up, no doubt assessing where Nick would fall in the unspoken department hierarchy. Every place had one. Nick's first impression was that Kent placed himself pretty high on that chart. His second impression: he and Kent were not going to be best friends.

Nick wasn't interested in getting into a discussion about his previous job or his motivation for transfer, not at this point. No doubt the team had already been briefed on his arrival and probably provided some pertinent details. That was enough for now. He was a proponent of the 'need to know' philosophy, and at that moment, Kent did not need to know.

"Yes, it is," he answered politely. "Nice to meet you, Kent. If you'll excuse me, I don't want to keep the chief waiting."

Walking toward the office at the back, Nick nodded acknowledgements to the other two occupants who, unlike Kent, appeared to be busy and didn't feel the need for an immediate intro. That worked for him.

The chief's door was open, so Nick knocked lightly on the frame. The big guy behind the desk looked up from the report he was reading, his mouth forming a wide smile when he saw Nick. "Nick Benning! About time you got your ass back here! Come on in, son, and close the door behind you."

Nick turned to close the door. As he did, he saw Kent watching the exchange with undisguised interest.

"Don't mind Kent," Sam told him, now standing. "Likes to pretend he's the alpha dog, but he's the only one who thinks so."

Nick chuckled, feeling some of the tension in his shoulders easing. About fifty, Sam Brown was a big guy. His dark hair was peppered with silver, his dark brown eyes sharp and assessing. Judging by the small creases around his eyes and mouth, the man smiled and laughed often.

Chief Brown indicated he should take a seat, then got right into it.

"What happened is a matter of public record," Sam told him, "but as far as I'm concerned, it has nothing to do with your role in this department. You're coming in here as a good cop, and I've been singing your praises as such."

Nick appreciated his candor, but like the chief said, what happened all those years ago was a matter of public record, accessible to anyone who had a mind to do some digging. If someone brought it up or it became a problem, he'd address it.

"I don't expect any problems. Eve's finally getting the help she needs and on the advice of counsel, the family is keeping things as quiet and low-key as possible, but I won't lie. Image is a big thing with the Sandersons and they've turned pointing fingers into an art form. Best to be prepared, just in case."

Nick nodded somberly. He knew all about the wealthy, powerful family and their refusal to acknowledge anything that might taint their 'pristine' reputation among the local community. Drug use and mental illness weren't things they wanted associated with the Sanderson name and they went to great lengths to secure those skeletons in deep, dark closets.

With that out of the way, they went over responsibilities and expectations. Covendale wasn't exactly a hotbed of criminal activity, but it had its share of problems. Given the recent rise in casual drug use among teenagers and young adults and Nick's record in dealing with such, he would be specializing in that area. They were a small department, though, so Sam told him that he could expect to work on just about anything that came up. That was fine with Nick. Keeping busy kept him focused and grounded.

Business preliminaries complete, Nick thanked the chief and stood up to go. Sam told him about the barbecue, insisting that it was just a casual thing, no big deal. When Nick agreed, Sam asked where he was staying and Nick told him about Gail's offer to help him find potential living arrangements.

"I knew you were a smart man," Sam said on a laugh. "Best just to accept her help with grace, because you're going to get it anyway."

Sam introduced him to the two others he'd seen earlier, Joe Hibbs and Cybil Galligan, both of whom seemed like decent folk. Reserved, assessing. Nick pegged them as the kind of people who quietly got the job done and weren't all about the accolades (unlike Emerson). He liked them instantly.

The rest of the morning was spent filling out paperwork and setting up his accounts in the computer system. Then there was the "welcome to the department" lunch at Lou's (which he appreciated), and an afternoon of getting acquainted with some of the cases he'd be working on. All in all, it was a good first day and by the time he left, he already felt at home.

Nick grabbed a quick bite to eat, then tried Liz's number again. When it went to voicemail, he hung up and dialed Gail's sister. Marianne Keller told him she'd been expecting his call. He explained that he was looking for a place to lease initially. She asked him some general questions about location, price, and preferences, then promised to have a list of potential places for him to check out as soon as possible.

He took advantage of the free time to pick up a few things and drove around a bit more, reacclimating himself to the small town where he'd grown up. Memories flooded back, some good, some not so good. There was the salvage yard where he and his father used to scavenge for parts for the Shelby. The bridge along the river where he and his friends used to hang out after high-school. The scenic overlook where he and Annie had first discovered the wonders of sex. Finally, he drove to the cemetery.

He ran his hands over the smooth marble headstone that marked the grave of his Annie. "Hey, baby," he spoke quietly. "Sorry it's been so long."

Thinking of her still hurt, though time had worn the pain down into more of a dull ache than the ragged, slicing blade it had once been. Annie had been his first love, and he, hers. They'd been so young then, so naïve, believing they had their whole lives ahead of them.

Now he knew better. Nothing was guaranteed. Not today, not tomorrow. All anyone had was *right now*, and it was what they chose to do with it that was the important thing.

Chapter Two

~ *Mack* ~

"Please, Mack," her father pleaded over the phone.

Heather "Mack" MacKenzie pulled the phone away from her ear and stared at it. He was kidding, right? He couldn't really be asking her to babysit the brat, could he?

"She is twenty-seven years old, Dad. She's not a child."

"No," he agreed, sounding much older and wearier than the last time they had spoken. No surprise there. Dealing with her spoiled stepsister was enough to suck the life force out of anyone, even someone as vibrant as her father. She felt a stab of sympathy for him, but it passed quickly. Choices, and all that.

"But she isn't exactly mature, either," he continued. "She needs to learn how to do for herself. Catherine can't say no to her. It's becoming a point of contention between us and putting a strain on our marriage."

Let it, Mack wanted to say. *Ditch the dead weight and come stay with me.* Instead she said, "So you want to send her to *me*?"

The skepticism in her voice was obvious; she and Dee had never gotten along. Mack tried to picture the well-coiffed former deb in her rustic, eco-friendly home and failed. When Mack had fallen in love with the sprawling, spacious house, she never once imagined Princess Dee stepping over the threshold.

"You're a good role model, Mack. Strong and independent. You won't coddle her."

Not coddle her? Dee would be lucky if Mack didn't murder her in her sleep. As one of *the few, the proud* Mack knew about a hundred ways to do so while making it look like an accident. Her father knew this.

Or maybe he didn't. They didn't talk about that part of her life much. He hadn't exactly been thrilled when she'd enlisted the day after her eighteenth birthday, nor when she'd re-enlisted for an additional tour after that. The 'don't ask, don't tell' philosophy worked well for them.

"She's agreed to this?" Mack asked doubtfully.

George cleared his throat and hesitated, making the hairs on the back of her neck prickle in warning. "We're not giving her a choice. Catherine and I are going abroad. Alone.'"

Mack mentally translated that to a big, fat "no", which meant that Princess Dee wasn't any happier with the idea than she was. The only thing worse than an unwanted houseguest was an unwanted houseguest who didn't want to be there, either.

"We'll provide an allowance to help with basic expenses, but it will be much less than what she is used to and will go directly to you to disburse as you see fit."

It was on the tip of Mack's tongue to tell her father that she neither needed nor wanted his money, but then thought better of it. He *should* pay something for what he was asking. Mack started making a mental list of the local organizations that might benefit from her father's restitutions and her personal sacrifice. She scribbled 'animal rescue' and 'women's shelter' on the notepad beside the slim desktop monitor.

"She's not going to like that. Especially the 'much less than what she's used to' part."

"No," he agreed, "but that will provide incentive for her to get a job."

Mack snorted. "A job doing what, exactly?" As far as she knew, Dee wasn't qualified to do anything besides bat her eyes and point a well-manicured finger, expecting everyone to do her bidding.

Another long pause told her everything she needed to know. Mack let out a heavy sigh. "You're kidding, right?" Mack rubbed at the dull ache blossoming between her eyes. "There must be something she can do. Didn't she go to that fancy college?"

"For a while, yes," her father said slowly, "but we stopped paying her tuition when she failed all of her classes. Catherine sent her to quite a few modeling and dance schools, though, when she was younger. Maybe you could find something for her at *Seize*. You have dance fitness classes, right?"

Jesus, give me strength. The conversation just kept getting better. Now her father was not only asking Mack to share her home, but to give Dee a job as well? In her fitness center! *Seize* was Mack's baby. It was her pride, her life, built on things like discipline and a desire to improve oneself — concepts that were completely foreign to Dee's self-absorbed, pampered existence.

"Please, Heather," her father said after long minutes stretched in silence, pulling Mack out of her musings. *No one* called her Heather, not since her mother had passed away. The situation had to be even worse than she'd thought if he was pulling that shit.

"You know I wouldn't ask if there was another option," he confirmed. "It's just for a couple weeks, a few months, tops. Once we have the Copenhagen office up and running and our marriage back on track, we'll be back to take her off your hands."

God. Damn. It. She was going to say yes. She

couldn't deny him; the man rarely asked for anything. She might as well get SUCKER tattooed on her forehead. If nothing else, it could hide the bruises she'd get from banging her head against the wall. Mack closed her eyes and sighed heavily. "All right, Dad."

His sigh of relief was audible. "I won't forget this, baby."

"Yeah, I know. When is she coming?" Mack started a new list, all the things she'd have to do before the Princess's arrival. She had a spare guest room, but she'd need to get some bedding and pillows ready and —

"Her flight's getting into Philly tonight. We've arranged for a car to drive her to Covendale."

"She's coming *tonight*?!"

The dread that had been building in her belly since the beginning of their conversation exploded. Mack laughed through the sudden urge to lay waste to everything around her. *Crafty old codger.* "You knew I would say yes, didn't you?"

"I knew my baby wouldn't let me down," he affirmed, managing to imbue enough affection in those few words to have her eyes tearing up. That kind of pissed her off, because Mack *never* cried. "I love you, baby."

"I love you, too, Daddy."

Mack hung up the phone and inhaled deeply, held her breath for several seconds, then let it out. Then she did it again. And again. Until she could keep the torrent of unladylike curses from being readily audible by anyone not within a ten foot radius. As the owner of *Seize* — the premier fitness center for miles around — she needed to show more professionalism than that.

Pfft, her inner voice scoffed. No one who knew her would be surprised if she let a couple f-bombs drop. But she held them in anyway.

She briefly considered locking herself in her office, closing the blinds, and hiding before anything else reared up and bit her on the ass. First, her morning receptionist Chrissy decided to elope without warning, leaving the front desk unstaffed, and now Evil Princess Dee was flying into town (quite possibly on a broom) and Mack had to figure out what to do with her for the next couple of weeks.

Clearly, fate was feeling salty. What other surprises would this day have in store for her?

Chapter Three

~ *Nick* ~

"Excuse me." The woman at the semi-circular front desk didn't appear to have heard him. Turned slightly away from him as she was, he couldn't quite make out her facial features. It took him a minute to realize she was on the phone. Nick waited patiently, taking the opportunity to check out the place out.

According to Gail, many of the men and women who made up the local law enforcement were members and spoke very highly of it. *Seize* was on the short list of places she recommended he check out. Not only would it give him a place to stay in shape, but according to Gail, it also had an active teen and pre-teen program that could prove mutually beneficial. Nick believed that a huge part of reducing drug use — and thus drug-related deaths and crimes — was providing education, positive role models, and viable alternatives for kids. Getting involved with the schools was a given, but what about the summer months, when so many kids had less adult supervision and more time on their hands? If he established a rapport and built trust with the kids here as well as through district programs, the probability of making a difference rose dramatically.

He hummed in approval at the tinted, floor-to-ceiling panel windows along the front. It gave the place an open, airy feel, which he liked. A large white ceiling fan circulated lazily above an assortment of plants, some exotic, some not. The faint scent of lemons hung in the air.

Overall impression: clean, functional, and exactly the kind of place he was looking for.

First inspection complete, he turned his attention back to the woman behind the desk. Nick used his finely-honed skills of observation to silently appreciate the sun-kissed, satiny skin stretched tight over well-toned arms. Dark chestnut hair pulled up in a ponytail revealed a tiny, heart-shaped white birthmark behind her left ear. Petite as she was, there was nothing delicate about her. She radiated strength and energy.

And at that moment, irritation.

"No, Jay," she said on an exhale. "*Tonight,* can you believe it?... Yeah... You sure you're okay with this?... You are a saint... No, three hundred thread count is more than enough… Yeah, I know… Bye, gorgeous." She put down the phone and Nick could have sworn she *growled*.

Her call completed, Nick cleared his throat and repeated the phrase a second time before she turned his way. For a moment, he felt as if a pair of lasers were directed right at his heart. Pale gray-green eyes locked on him, doing a complete assessment in the matter of a second or two. Then she blinked and that feral expression smoothed into a pleasant, professional mask.

"I'm sorry about that. Can I help you?"

For a moment, his mind went blank. Dressed in skin-tight black yoga pants and black sports tank, she was even more attractive standing up. Thankfully, his brain kicked back into gear before she pegged him as a slack-jawed idiot.

"I hope so. I'm looking for a place to work out. *Seize* came highly recommended."

"Of course," she said, relaxing enough to offer him an easy smile. She waved him into the small, functional office to the right. "Come on in. My name's Mack."

"Mack?" She didn't look like a Mack. "Mack" conjured visions of big, beefy, tattooed truck drivers or dock workers. This creature before him was one hundred percent concentrated female.

"Short for MacKenzie," she explained.

"Nick Benning," he said, accepting her hand. It was so much smaller than his, but strong and warm.

And he'd been right about her being tiny; standing, she barely reached his chin.

She stepped back and looked him up and down, her gaze professionally assessing. "Cop?" she asked.

"Detective. How'd you know?"

She shrugged, a graceful lift of her shoulders. "We have lots of local boys here. Is that how you heard about *Seize*?"

It had been a long time since anyone had called him a boy, but he didn't take offense. She wasn't any older than he was and her tone held admiration, not disrespect.

"The police chief's wife, actually."

Her lips curled into a genuine smile. "Gail is one of my biggest promoters. I'm going to have to start paying her referral fees. So, you're new in town?"

"I just transferred from Chicago." He resisted the temptation to explain that he'd been born and raised in Covendale. He wasn't, by nature, a sharer, and years on the force had cemented the wisdom of not providing more information than necessary. He waited for her to pump him for more details, but she didn't.

Instead, she simply nodded. "We offer two-week trials, free of charge. Unlimited use of the facilities. We're open from five a.m. till midnight, seven days a week."

"That's a lot of hours."

"Many of our members work crazy shifts and don't get weekends off," she shrugged, as if every business was as accommodating. "We have a couple of weight rooms — free weights, Stride, Nautilus — plus a full cardio deck. Heated Olympic in-ground pool. Massage rooms, saunas, steam rooms. Group classes in everything from meditation to MMA."

"Sounds great."

"It is," she nodded without any trace of arrogance. A couple of teens ran past the office and waved, shouting out 'heys' to her, which she returned with a genuine smile and a wave of her own. "We also have a day care and a teen center, as well as several programs aimed at providing positive options, if you have kids." Her eyes drifted down to his left hand.

"I don't," he said simply. Was she fishing? Or just providing information? Her pretty eyes gave nothing away. He liked that. Being a detective, he'd become adept at reading people. But Mack, she was making him work for it. "I'm not married."

Her eyes flashed for just a moment—interest, maybe?—before she continued. "We have a small onsite canteen, too, stocked with healthy, organic snacks and smoothies if you need to refuel."

"So… if I want a burger and fries…?" he teased.

The corner of her mouth twitched. "You'll have to hit Lou's. But that's okay. We get a lot of new members that way."

She turned away and leaned over the desk, offering him an unobstructed view of her toned, nicely curved ass. Nick caught himself staring, then shoved his hands into his pockets and focused his attention on the leafy green plant/tree in the corner. What was wrong with him? First, he's sharing personal info, then he's ogling her like they're in high school or something. It was a little unsettling. And kind of arousing. How long had it been since he'd had such an instant, *positive* reaction to anyone?

Slow your roll, Benning, he told himself. *Just because you've decided to wander beyond your own self-imposed fence doesn't mean you have to go pissing on every bush you see.*

"Here's a temporary key card and a brochure that explains everything. We've got an app you can download, too," she said, straightening and turning back around to face him. She was looking at him expectantly, and he realized she was holding something out to him. Nick took it, his fingers brushing hers lightly in the process. She didn't seem to notice, using her free hand to summon someone behind him. He frowned, irrationally annoyed with whoever was taking her attention away from him.

"The key card is good for the two-week trial," she continued. "If you decide to join, we'll issue you a permanent photo id and take your money." She flashed him a grin that sent tiny sparks firing simultaneously in his chest and his groin.

"This is Carl," she said, nodding to someone behind him. The new arrival entered the office and positioned himself next to Mack. Carl turned out to be a lean, muscular guy sporting a polo with the gym's logo. In an instant, the strange fog clouding his rational thought processes cleared and Nick felt more like himself again.

"Carl, this is Detective Benning. Carl is in charge of our wellness programs. He can give you the grand tour and answer all of your questions. Sorry I can't do it myself, but we're a little shorthanded today."

Strangely disappointed that Mack wouldn't be giving him the tour, he shook Carl's hand. As he did, Mack stiffened, her expression going from friendly and welcoming to instantly guarded as she once again looked past him. Nick turned to find out why and found a tall, svelte blonde ogling his backside appreciatively.

"Hello," the blonde purred.

"Hello," he said, his smile faded as quickly as Mack's had.

"*Delilah*." The low female growl came from Mack holding no trace of the warmth it had only seconds earlier. "Thought you weren't getting in until later tonight."

"I got an earlier flight," the leggy blonde said, shifting her weight skillfully to accentuate her sleek form without bothering to glance over in Mack's direction.

"Fucking awesome," he heard Mack mutter, pulling him back from the dark thoughts that had started rolling in. He suppressed the smile that tried to take hold.

"Carl was just about to show Nick around. You can wait in my office." Mack told her.

"Oh? Mind if I tag along?" Dee asked, fluttering her eyes. She didn't give Nick a chance to answer before she slipped her hand around his bicep and made an appreciative noise.

Nick gently but firmly removed her hand. Chancing a glance at Mack, he saw her with hands on hips, body tense, and little flames in those pretty gray-green eyes. Clearly, she wasn't any more pleased with the situation than he was.

Mack's gaze met his, and something passed between them. He knew in that moment that she understood. "*I* mind," she said firmly. "Carl, give Detective Benning the grand tour. Dee, you and I have a few things to discuss."

"Follow me." As Carl led him away, Nick chanced a quick, appreciative glance over his shoulder. Mack offered a quick nod of acknowledgement. Something told him he was really going to like it here.

Chapter Four

~ Mack ~

Mack felt the last of her good humor drain away as Carl led Detective Benning away. Dee wasn't even trying to hide the fact that she was checking out his ass. Granted, the detective did have a nice ass, as well as nice hands, shoulders, and smile, but Mack had zero tolerance when it came to harassment. She wanted *Seize* to be a safe zone and she wanted her members—men as well as women—to feel comfortable there.

"Delilah." Even with her sharp tone, her stepsister had trouble tearing her eyes away. "Roll that tongue back into your mouth. Rule #1: we do not ogle, flirt with, or proposition clients."

Delilah's ruby red lips formed a perfect (and well-practiced) pout. "What's the use of being surrounded by beefcake if you can't have a nibble?"

"When you're here, you're a vegetarian. Got

it?"

The pout morphed to a scowl. "You never were any fun."

"And you've always been obsessed with the opposite sex."

"You say that like it's a bad thing."

The dull throb at the base of her skull intensified. Mack loved her father, but really, what the hell had he been thinking when he hooked up with Catherine Barrington and her demon spawn?

Catherine was *nothing* like Mack's mom. Mack's mom had been loving and sweet, always ready with a freshly baked cookie and a warm hug at the end of the day, right up until the time she died. Short and ample with laughing blue eyes and a ready smile, she had simply been a beautiful person inside and out.

In contrast, Catherine was tall and slender with all the warmth of an icicle. Any hint of laugh lines was dealt with swiftly and severely; Catherine's father was an internationally heralded plastic surgeon, after all. Mack doubted the woman had ever touched a cookie in her life, let alone baked one.

Catherine's daughter, Delilah, was a real-life example of the apple not falling far from the tree. Mack and Delilah were as different as night and day. Tall, slim, blonde, and vain, Delilah's sole ambition in life was finding a wealthy man to take care of her so she didn't have to lift a finger.

Except, of course, to have it manicured.

And why wouldn't she? That plan had worked well for Dee's mother. Mack's father was husband number three, and with him, Catherine had hit the mother lode.

The familiar anger simmered low in her belly. Mack was so used to it by now that it barely even registered. Anger at Catherine for being a gold-digger and taking advantage of a lonely man. Anger at Delilah for being such a spoiled, prissy little brat. Anger at her father for not seeing Catherine for what she really was and for bringing that woman and her daughter into *their* house.

The mother-daughter duo was one of the main reasons she'd joined the Marines, to get away from all that. From them. Despite her father's dire warnings, she hadn't regretted a single minute of it. Signing up had been the best thing she'd ever done, next to opening *Seize*. Now, here she was, more than ten years later and on the other side of the country, *still* having to deal with their shit.

If only she'd let the call go to voicemail. But she'd seen her dad's number pop up and secretly hoped he was calling to say he'd finally seen the light and was flying out for a visit to see her and the new fitness center, the one she'd been pouring her heart and soul into for the past couple of years. She'd named the place *Seize*, inspired by her favorite saying—*carpe diem*—and the ideal of providing an affordable opportunity for people to take control of their life in terms of health, fitness, and discipline like she had.

Not only was her father not coming, but she was stuck with Delilah for an indeterminate amount of time ranging anywhere from weeks to months. How was she going to pull it off? Not even two minutes into her stepsister's arrival and she already regretted agreeing to her father's request. The next few weeks were going to *suck.*

Mack exhaled heavily and summoned her patience. One of the reasons her father wanted her to look after Dee was to provide a good example of responsibility and maturity, although the realist in her knew it was probably more a case of no one else being able to tolerate Dee for any length of time.

"All right. You're here, so we might as well make the best of it. We'll get you settled in at my place tonight and you can start first thing in the morning. What can you do?"

"Excuse me?"

"What job skills do you have?"

Delilah stared blankly back at her, and Mack realized her father had selectively omitted that little nugget about getting a job when he'd been shoving Dee's ass on the plane.

"While you are staying with me, you *will* be working here."

Dee laughed, then sobered when she realized Mack was serious. "You're joking."

"No. This isn't not a brief weekend visit, Dee.

If you're going to be living in my house, I expect you to earn your keep."

Dee's eyes narrowed. "Doing what?"

"Let's start simple. Can you answer the phone? Use a computer?"

Dee sniffed, looking down her perfect, surgically sculpted nose. "I suppose."

"Great. You're my new receptionist until Chrissy gets back from her honeymoon. Grab a seat and I'll give you a quick how-to."

"What, right *now*?"

"No time like the present."

"But I just got here!"

"I won't have time to show you in the morning."

"Don't I get a tour, too? I mean, if I'm going to work here—" her face scrunched up as if she'd just sucked on a lemon "—then I should at least be familiar with the place, right?"

From a normal job applicant, that would make perfect sense, but this was Dee, and there were only two reasons why Princess Dee would want a tour. One was, she wanted to avoid work and the other was, she wanted to scope out more guys. Both were equally probable and neither was acceptable.

"Tomorrow, when Margo comes in to take over, I'll give you the grand tour."

Mack demonstrated how to use the phone system to answer and transfer calls, as well as put people on and off hold. She also showed her the basics of the computer system so that Dee would be able to answer simple questions about hours, classes, and membership.

"Be pleasant, professional, and respectful to everyone. It's all pretty simple and straightforward. If there's something you can't handle or answer, take their name and number and tell them I'll get back to them shortly," Mack concluded about thirty minutes later. "Now, let's get you back to my place. I'm sure you're tired and five a.m. comes early."

"Make it two. I don't get up until at least eleven."

God, give me strength.

Chapter Five

~ *Nick* ~

"So, what are your fitness goals?" Carl asked as they pushed through a set of double insulated glass doors. "Strength? Endurance? MMA?"

Carl's question brought Nick's mind back to the present. The blonde's bold actions had dredged up some unpleasant memories of another woman, one he didn't care to remember. He shook them off, reminding himself that not all beautiful, bold women were crazies like Eve Sanderson. Regardless, he still held a strong personal dislike for the type and made a mental note to keep his distance.

"Strength and cardio, mostly, but MMA sounds interesting."

"It's not for everyone." Carl gave Nick an

assessing once-over as they moved. "Ever try it?"

"I know some basics, mostly self-defense and disarming techniques."

"That's a good start. We can build on that. I teach a couple of classes. When we're done with the tour, I'll grab a schedule for you. We encourage people to try new things, step outside their comfort zone. Membership gives you a free pass to everything *Seize* has to offer, no added fees, no hidden agenda. That includes use of all facilities, equipment, and classes, as well as one-on-one coaching."

"Sounds great."

"We believe that keeping things fresh and fun is the key to long lasting fitness."

Carl took him through the facility, which looked new and well-maintained. The workout areas were clean and spacious with a staggering assortment of state-of-the-art equipment to choose from.

"You sure have a lot of options," Nick commented as they moved from the group training rooms to the pool, where an aquatic spinning class was in the shallow end. On the far side, several lanes had been roped off for lap swimming.

"Fitness is a very personal thing, Detective. We've got something for everyone, from hardcore professionals to senior citizen groups. There is no one-size-fits-all option. Our goal is to promote health and wellbeing at any level."

They ended the tour back where they'd started, near the main entrance. Mack wasn't there, which Nick found disappointing. "So, what do you think?"

"I think it's great," Nick answered honestly.

Carl nodded, as if that was the reaction he'd expected. "We've got a lot of cops here. Firefighters, too. Did Mack tell you about the service discount?"

"No, we hadn't gotten that far."

"Ah, well, Mack's real big on giving back to the community. Public servants get a twenty-five percent discount."

"How does the owner feel about that?"

Carl laughed. "Mack *is* the owner."

Nick's surprise must have shown, because Carl added, "Don't worry, you're not the first to make the wrong assumption." Carl gave him a schedule and wrote his name and number across the top. "If you have any questions, give me a call."

"I will, thanks." Nick agreed to the two-week trial, but he'd already made up his mind. *Seize* was definitely the place for him.

~ * ~

Driving to the Chief's house on Saturday afternoon, Nick's thoughts roamed back to the intriguing owner of *Seize*. It wasn't the first time. Images of those flashing eyes and smirking lips — the ones that suggested she knew something he didn't — had been popping into his mind repeatedly.

What was her story, he wondered? She had an interesting one, of that he was certain. Where had she come from and what made her decide to set up shop in Covendale? Did she have family in the area? Was she involved with anyone?

More importantly, why couldn't he stop thinking about her?

Only one other woman had managed to hijack his thoughts so quick and thoroughly. Freshman year of high school. Second period. Mr. Kartofski's earth science lab. He remembered it as if it was yesterday. Annie Sullivan had smiled at him from across the room and he'd been lost.

He sighed. He was getting ahead of himself. He wasn't that same awkward, hormone-riddled adolescent he'd been then; he was a fully-grown man with too much life experience under his belt to go jumping to conclusions. That flash in her eyes might have been nothing more than a trick of the light and perhaps some subconscious, wishful thinking on his part. Maybe she wasn't even interested.

But what if she was? Now that he was moving forward again, wasn't the possibility worth investigating?

'Maybe' was the best answer he could come up with. Instant chemistry or not, he'd been out of the game for a long time and it was quite possible he was totally misreading the situation. Bottom line: he needed to proceed with caution.

That decided, he turned his thoughts to the present. He found a parking place on the street around the block and took a deep breath, preparing himself for an afternoon of being 'the new guy'. Even though his family had been in the area for decades, *he* hadn't been, and it was as good a place as any to start re-introducing himself to the community.

There was already a decent-sized crowd at Chief Brown's when he arrived. Gail greeted him with a warm, friendly smile and immediately took him out back where most of the action was. Nick recognized some guests from the station. Kent Emerson was there, as well as Joe Hibbs and Cybil Galligan and half a dozen guys he pegged as uniforms. Many appeared to have come with spouses and kids. A few, like Emerson, had a plus one. Others, like him, were flying solo. Some looked vaguely familiar, as if he might have gone to school with them or seen them around the garage where he worked during the summers.

The chief waved him over to one of the largest outdoor grills Nick had ever seen, waving a spatula toward a massive tub of ice filled with bottles of beer and soda. "Glad you made it! Help yourself."

"Thanks. Nice grill."

Sam beamed with pride. "This here's the Flame Master 5000. Best grill money can buy and envy of every man here. Not that I'll let any of them near it," he said on a laugh.

Nick grabbed a beer and twisted off the top and looked around, feeling some of the tension ebb away. He'd missed these kinds of cookouts. When he'd been growing up, barely a summer weekend had gone by without his parents or one of their neighbors having one. Adults would talk and chill and the kids would spend all day running around, splashing in the pool, grabbing ice pops, then lighting sparklers and catching lightning bugs at night until their parents dragged them home. They were good memories.

Gail reappeared with a plate piled high with hamburger and hot dog buns and set them down on a table near the grill. "Come on, Nick, let me introduce you around."

"Behave yourself," Sam warned her, then looked at Nick and lowered his voice. "My Gail is a notorious matchmaker."

"Oh, go on with you," Gail waved her husband off, but her eyes were twinkling. "I'm just being neighborly. Anything else is up to fate."

"Fate, huh?" Nick chuckled as Gail looped her arm through his and led him away from Sam and his Flame Master 5000.

"Absolutely. I'm a strong believer in fate. There's a reason you came back to us now," she told him.

An image of Mack flashed in his mind. "Yeah,

what's that?"

She laughed softly. "Darned if I know. Despite what Sam says, I'm not a meddler. All I'm saying is, keep your head and heart open to the possibilities and everything will work out."

They approached a couple, mid-fortyish, sitting comfortably in large deck chairs beneath the canopy that had been set up. "Nick, this is my sister, Marianne and her husband, Tom Keller. Marianne, Tom, Nick Benning."

Both rose to greet him. "Nick! So good to meet you in person!" Marianne said as Nick shook hands with Tom. "I was hoping to see you here. I think I've found the perfect place for you."

Nick lifted his brows in surprise. "Already?"

"It's a terrific Cape Cod on the edge of town, two acres, garage, and ready for immediate occupancy. The owners moved rather quickly; the husband got a temporary transfer to North Carolina to help set up a new office and they're looking to lease the place out for the cost of the monthly mortgage payment. It comes furnished with the basics, but they've already put most of their stuff in storage, so it won't feel too weird. We can look at it as soon as tomorrow, if that works for you."

She paused to take a breath and her husband laughed. "You'll have to forgive my wife's enthusiasm."

Nick laughed, too. "No problem. It's nice to meet someone who loves what they do. And tomorrow would be great, thanks."

The rest of the afternoon passed pleasantly enough. People were polite and friendly, though he did catch the curious glances and occasional whispers. It wasn't unexpected. Covendale was a small-town community, and small-town communities tended to have long memories.

Proof of that came later as Nick made his way into the house to seek out the bathroom.

"So, what do you think of the new guy?" Nick paused in the kitchen, recognizing the voice of the redhead who'd been hanging around Emerson.

"He seems nice. He's got that whole "still waters run deep" vibe going on, which is kind of sexy. Don't tell Joe I said so, though."

Emerson's date — Nick thought her name was Cameron — laughed. "Agreed."

Nick pegged the other woman as Stacy Hibbs, Joe's wife.

As much as his male ego enjoyed hearing that, eavesdropping on a private conversation wasn't his thing. Nick was just about to backtrack when Cameron's next words made him hesitate. "Kent says the guy has some dark history here."

The other woman said nothing.

"Something about a big scandal," Emerson's date pushed, "and that Nick skipped town after his fiancée died."

"It wasn't like that." Stacy said quietly. "And Kent wasn't even around then."

"No, but Kent said—"

"Look, Cameron," Stacy's voice was quiet, yet firm. "I don't mean to be rude, but Kent shouldn't be talking about things he knows nothing about, and you shouldn't believe everything you hear."

The redhead stormed out of the bathroom and made a beeline for the patio. Stacy came out a few moments later and spotted him. Genuine sympathy crossed over her features.

"You heard that, didn't you? I'm sorry. Some people don't know when to keep their big mouths shut."

Nick nodded. Stacy wasn't wrong. "Thanks."

"You don't remember me, do you?"

"No, I'm sorry."

"We went to high school together. I was Stacy Leonard then."

Nick searched his memories for the name, coming up with a picture of a skinny girl with thick glasses and braces, but it was hard to reconcile that image with the slightly plump, radiant-faced beauty standing next to him now. "Ms. Opelka's algebra class, right?"

Her smile was brilliant and genuine. "You do remember!"

"I do now, but in my defense, you look a little different now than you did then."

She laughed. "Contact lenses and three kids will do that to you. Listen, can I give you a piece of friendly, unsolicited advice?" Nick nodded. "Watch your back around Kent, okay?"

Nick had already figured that out. Though Kent was outwardly friendly when others were around, Nick kept picking up a distinctly *un*friendly vibe, one that seemed to extend beyond simple office politics. It felt personal, which didn't make any sense. Nick hadn't even met the guy until a week ago.

"Yeah. It's the *why* of it that eludes me."

Stacy's eyes widened. "You don't know? Kent Emerson is Eve Sanderson's cousin."

Well, that explained a lot. "No, I didn't know that, but thanks for the heads-up."

Chapter Six

~ *Mack* ~

"Why are you eating dried ball sacks?"

Mack glanced up from the table to see her housemate, Jay, looking at her with an expression of abject horror.

"They are *not* dried ball sacks," she huffed. "They're organic Turkish figs." She held up the container so he could read the label. They didn't hold the same comfort factor as warm, fresh-from-the-oven chocolate chip cookies, but they were sweet and rich enough to be a viable, healthy alternative when a quick fix was needed.

After dealing with Delilah, she needed all the sweet, comforting richness her organic diet would allow. When she wasn't prying her man-crazy stepsister away from attractive male members, she was trying to teach her enough basic Receptionist

101 stuff to make her passably useful. It had barely been a week and Mack was already toying with the idea of drugging Dee and putting her ass on a plane. She had even gone as far as calling the airport, but the man at the ticket counter hung up when she asked when the next flight to 'somewhere far away and hostile' was.

Jay scrunched his perfectly straight Grecian nose, his smoldering hazel eyes suspicious. "They *look* like dried ball sacks."

Leaning against the doorframe and wearing nothing more than a pair of board shorts on his slim hips and showcasing an impressive V of roped male muscle, Jay would have had most women panting. However, because Jay was Mack's best friend—and because he was one hundred percent gay—she barely noticed beyond an appreciative glance. Half the women who joined her gym the year before did so after Jay was featured in a popular men's underwear ad and credited Mack for his healthy diet and exercise program.

"Hmmm," Mack hummed, holding the fruit in her palm and studying it. "You're right. Never noticed that before." She took a bite and rolled her eyes back in her head. "Delicious."

Jay winced, his lightly bronzed face turning abnormally pale as he instinctively covered his crotch. "You are a vicious, vicious woman. No wonder you're sitting home alone on a Saturday night."

Mack stuck her tongue out at him. Given what she was chewing at the time, it was not a pretty sight.

"Ew, Mack. Just ew. And what's got you horking carbs anyway?"

She shot him a venomous look that could have singed the hair from his body, assuming he had any. As a male model, his skin was nothing but a smooth, pristine canvas. A lesser woman might have been jealous of just how perfect his skin was.

"Oh, right," he laughed. "Spa day. How'd it go?"

Mack growled at him. In a goodwill effort of superhuman proportions, Mack had reluctantly taken a few hours off to spend with her stepsister, kind of a "you're here, let's make the best of it" gesture. If she'd had half a brain, she would have just left Dee at the salon/spa and gone back to work. But no. She'd felt compelled to try and find some common ground.

Well, she wouldn't have to worry about doing that again.

"I've been banned."

Jay laughed harder. "How did you manage that? And hey, are those my boxers you're wearing?"

Mack felt the heat rush to her face. "No," she lied, tugging guiltily at the black silk. Men's underwear was comfortable and roomy, while women's underwear was skimpy and not. Who in their right mind decided that scratchy lace and dental floss would feel good against such a sensitive area, she wanted to know? *Especially* after a wax.

"You might as well tell me, Mack. Don't make me call Marcus and get the scoop from him."

Mack looked everywhere but at Jay. "I *might* have kicked the aesthetician in the face when she pulled a wax strip from my bikini line."

Trying to cover his mouth, he snickered, "Mack, you didn't."

"'Fraid so," she sighed. "But that hurts, you know?"

"Yes, I know."

Jay was the best of the best. She could (and often did) confide things to him that she would have otherwise taken to her grave, which was why she kept talking instead of shutting up like she should have.

"It looked really odd, just having one bare patch, so I tried to, you know, even it out myself when I got home. Except I didn't have any wax, so..."

The true horror of the situation began to dawn on him. "Tell me you did not use your regular razor."

She blinked and looked up at him. "What else would I use?"

"Oh, baby girl. They make special small ones for that sort of thing." He waved his hand in the general area of her crotch.

"And how the hell would I know that?" she said, nearly shouting now.

"Because you're a woman. You're supposed to know that kind of stuff. It's like instinct or something. Didn't anyone teach you?"

She squirmed again. Maybe if her mother had lived long enough to see her through puberty, they might have had a chance to talk about those kinds of things. As it was, Mack had bumbled through a lot of self-discovery along the way. Proper feminine 'scaping techniques sure as hell weren't covered in basic training.

"I must have been absent that day," she mumbled.

"So… God, I can't believe I'm asking this … is everything, uh, okay down there?"

"As good as it's going to get."

Jay closed his eyes and pinched the bridge of his nose. Mack saw his lips silently counting to ten before speaking. "You need professional help. You know that, don't you?"

"Why? Because I can't fold myself in half and look at my lady parts?"

"Most people use a mirror," he mumbled before exhaling heavily. "Is there someone who can help you?"

Mack was horrified. "I'd rather paint my body in honey and lay on a mound of fire ants."

"There's a visual."

"Are you telling me you would be okay will

letting someone do that to you?"

He smirked. "How do you think I finally got Marcus to third base?"

Marcus was Jay's partner, an extremely talented hair and make-up artist with the modeling agency. The two had been seeing each other exclusively for several months and things were getting serious. Any day now Mack was expecting Jay to announce he was moving in with Marcus. She had already decided that if and when that happened, she would suggest that Marcus be the one to move into their house. There was more than enough room, and Mack didn't know what she would do without Jay to keep her sane and grounded.

Feeling even more depressed, Mack sighed and melted into Jay's embrace. He gave the best hugs.

"You'll find someone, baby girl," he said softly as he rubbed his hand up and down her back.

"Yeah," she snorted in disbelief.

"What about that hot new detective?"

She sat up, knowing immediately who he was referring to. "How do you know about him?"

"Honey, this is *Covendale*. A sexy, brooding alpha male rolls into town, people are going to notice. Tell me, what's he like?"

"How should I know?"

"Don't even try to pull that shit with me. I saw Carl giving him the tour, and no one gets in or out of *Seize* without you knowing about it. You met him, didn't you?"

"Sort of."

"Sort of?" he eyed her suspiciously. "What does that mean?"

She shrugged. "It means I talked to him for all of two minutes before Delilah showed up and started eye fucking him. I sent him off with Carl for his own safety."

"And sacrificed yourself in the process," Jay finished on a frustrated exhale.

She shrugged. "Delilah is *my* problem, not his. Besides, he's a potential client."

"He's a *hot* potential client. Maybe you and he…"

"*Pffft*. I don't think so. This —" she waved a hand over her face and body "— is not what guys dream about, you know?" It had been her experience that romantically speaking, most guys preferred women like Delilah: gorgeous, feminine, and easy. Easy on the eyes, easy on the intellect, easy on the effort. Intelligent, independent Marines made good girl *friends*, not good *girl*friends.

"Bullshit," Jay countered, reading her mind in that eerie way he had. "You need to adjust your attitude, get yourself out of the friend zone. It's like Purgatory — nowhere anyone wants to be. You need to stop having boy friends and get yourself a boyfriend, girlfriend."

"I've had boyfriends," she said defensively.

Jay snorted, somehow managing to make it

sound elegant.

"What about Mason?" she sniffed. "We went out a few times."

"Mason doesn't count."

"Why not?"

Sympathy turned to pity. "Hate to break it to you, baby girl, but Mason bats for my team."

"He does not!"

Jay smirked. "Mack, he has better fashion sense than Dee and likes to stick things up his ass."

Mack flushed a deep rose and averted her eyes. "Lots of men like to, uh, experiment that way. Stimulating the prostrate during sex can be very pleasurable."

Jay rolled his eyes. "Can you picture Mr. Tall and Yummy Detective sticking anything up *his* ass?"

Mack clamped her lips shut and reddened further. She refused to discuss Nick Benning or his really nice ass. Ever since she'd looked up to find the handsome detective in the office she hadn't been able to get him out of her mind. She *may* have even cast him a lead role in a late night fantasy or two. Typically, she tried to avoid incorporating people she had daily contact with into her private fantasies because it tended to make things weird, but Nick Benning was worth breaking a few unspoken rules for.

There was no way in hell she wanted anyone else to know, though. Not even Jay. Crushing on one of her clients would have to remain her dirty little secret.

"Seriously, Mack. Stop being an albatross and pull your head out of the sand."

"Ostrich," she mumbled, trying to pry her libidinous thoughts away from the detective's fine male behind.

"What?"

"*Ostriches* supposedly stick their head in the sand, not albatrosses... albatri? But even that's not true. It's a myth. I read this article in National Geographic..."

Jay gave her a withering look, the same one he gave her every time she started spouting useless geeky trivia. Mack wisely shut her mouth.

"All I'm saying is, it wouldn't hurt to release some of your inner diva."

"I think my inner diva was left behind in that spa, along with my dignity. There was screaming involved."

Jay sighed and pulled her into another hug. "Ah, Mack, what am I going to do with you? Come on, let's get you over to Marcus. He'll get you all fixed up."

"I'll pass, but thanks for the offer." Sliding carefully from her seat, Mack kissed his cheek before heading back toward her private bathroom to re-assess the damage.

With a mirror this time.

Chapter Seven

~ *Nick* ~

For a small town, Covendale had its fair share of temporary housing options, Nick thought as he looked at the short list of half a dozen places Maryann had emailed to him the night before. They'd made arrangements to meet up at the Cape Cod later that afternoon, but in the interests of thoroughness, she'd wanted him to know what else was available.

He appreciated the effort. To save time, he decided to do some drive-bys. Two he eliminated right off the bat; they were condos in town and Nick preferred something farther out. Of the remaining four, one was much bigger than what he was looking for, and another was in a cookie-cutter development popular with younger families.

The fifth house turned out to be a duplex, which wasn't a bad thing, but not his first choice.

He often worked odd hours depending on his cases, and he liked the quiet and privacy of a single home.

He'd saved the Cape Cod for last, and once he saw it, he knew right away why Marianne had chosen that one for a walk-through. It was exactly what he was looking for. An older place on the edge of town, the simple symmetry of the place appealed to him, as did the mullioned windows and classic shutters. The house looked in fairly good shape, and the property was large enough to have a nice buffer between the neighbors on either side. Eventually, he hoped to buy some land and build his own place, but until then, the Cape Cod would do quite nicely.

Nick swung by Liz's place again. She still hadn't returned any of his calls. He knew he had the right address; he'd double checked. Maybe her job required travel? Or perhaps she'd gone down to Florida to visit with their parents? Doing that was on his to-do list, right after he got settled. He was even thinking of asking Liz if she'd like to go with him. It had been a long time since the four of them had been together under one roof, and who knew how many more chances they'd have to do so.

A familiar pang of guilt went through his chest. He hoped his parents were okay. He'd done a shitty job of keeping in touch with them, too. At first, he called every holiday, but then his mom always brought up the past and started crying, asking him when he was coming home. His calls grew few and farther apart until he'd stopped calling all together.

At one point, Liz had expressed concern that their father was showing the beginning signs of Alzheimer's, but when she hadn't mentioned it again, he'd assumed everything was all right.

With some time to kill before he met Marianne at the house, Nick drove to Lou's and grabbed something quick for lunch. As he tipped the small bowl of coleslaw on top of his burger, he couldn't help but think about Mack's comment about burgers and fries sending people her way and smiled.

Something told him she was not a frequent patron of Lou's. Her body was too fit, too toned to enjoy the greasy burgers and sugary donuts he liked to indulge on occasionally.

Admittedly, his eating habits hadn't been the best. Working odd hours and living alone meant ease and convenience often won out over healthy and nutritious, though he tried to counteract that by running daily and working out when he could. He made a mental note to make regular trips to *Seize* part of his schedule. An added incentive to do so: more chances he'd run into Mack again. He was curious to see if he would feel the same unusual spark of interest as he had the first time, or if that had been just a fluke.

Popping the last French fry into his mouth, Nick wiped his hands on the napkin and counted out a generous tip for the server before heading back to the Cape Cod. Marianne pulled up to the curb a minute after he did. "I had a feeling you'd like this one," she said with a smile.

They walked around the inside. It needed a bit of work, but most of it was aesthetic. If it were his place, he'd slap on some new paint, do some minor refinishing, update the fixtures. The foundation was solid, the roof had been replaced less than ten years earlier, and there was no sign of water damage or infestation. On the surface, everything looked good.

The first floor had a nice-sized living room and kitchen, with a powder room and a mud/laundry room. The upstairs had two bedrooms, each with a nice dormer, and a shared full bath. The colors were neutral; the floorplan, simple.

"This is a good house," he commented as he checked out the partially finished basement.

"It is," she agreed.

The clincher was the two-bay garage at the rear of the property – plenty of room to set up shop and get back to one of his first loves: rebuilding classic muscle cars.

"So? What do you think?" Marianne asked when they reached the front door.

"I think," he said with a smile, "Gail was right. You do have a gift for finding people the perfect space."

Marianne smiled broadly, her cheeks flushing with color. "Thank you! I've got all the papers right here, but if you'd like to think about it for a few days, that's fine."

"No need. This is exactly what I had in mind

until the right parcel comes along. You'll help me with that, too, won't you?"

"I'd love to!"

"Then let's sign those papers."

Nick was in high spirits. Things were coming together nicely. Hoping to extend his lucky streak, he decided it was the perfect time to go work off that burger.

Chapter Eight

~ *Mack* ~

"God, Mack. How do you do it?"

Delilah flopped back on the L-shaped sectional, acting, for all intents and purposes, as if she'd been digging ditches in the heat all day instead of teaching one beginner Zumba class in a climate controlled, filtered-air studio and covering the reception desk for an hour. Sending Dee over to *Seize* for the Sunday morning class had been a stroke of genius, providing at least a few hours of Zen-like peace and quiet.

To be fair, Delilah had been *almost* bearable ever since the spa episode. Jay, good-hearted soul that he was, thought her good behavior was because she recognized that Mack had made a genuine effort to bridge the gap between them. Mack knew it was because Delilah was reliving Mack's humiliation over and over in her evil little mind and was simply laughing too hard to be her normal, horrible self.

"Do what, Dee? Work? It's a great way to pay bills and pass the time," Mack answered grumpily.

Dee snorted, somehow managing to make it sound feminine instead of the decidedly crass noise Mack made when she did it. When *she* snorted it sounded more like a pig snuffling for truffles. Mack wondered absently if Jay and Dee attended the same modelling school where they learned that kind of high-brow stuff.

"No. I mean spending all that time at the gym around so many hard-bodied hotties. How can you concentrate on *anything*?"

Oh, that. There *were* a lot of hot guys at the gym. Firefighters, cops, service men, and others whose jobs required them to be in peak physical condition had memberships. With its focus on total health, incorporating mind, body, and spirit, *Seize* had seen great success and its affordability made it a favorite among the public service crowd.

Not that Dee cared about any of that. She saw a set of glistening washboards and her mind went in one direction only: south.

"You know," Mack told her, pulling forth another nugget of trivia, "it's been scientifically proven that the scent of male sweat is calming to overstressed women."

Dee looked at her as if she was crazy. "Calming? Put me in with all that prime beef and that's the last thing I'm feeling. My lady parts tingle just thinking about it."

Mack felt offended on behalf of the "beef". Those men weren't cattle; they were hard-working guys who cared enough about themselves and the people they served to take care of their bodies, and it was her job to help them do it. And while Mack appreciated a toned, fit body as much as the next women, her lady parts didn't *tingle* at the sight.

With one notable exception.

As if picking up her thoughts, Dee added, "Especially the new guy, Nick. He is H-O-T."

Mack tensed at the easy way his name rolled off her tongue. Detective Benning was the only exception to her no-tingle rule, and Dee's mention brought forth flash images of her latest taboo fantasy. Something about the man made it hard to look at him as just a client. Maybe it was his kind eyes. Maybe it was his smile. Maybe it was the sense that there was so much more to discover beneath the disciplined, professional exterior.

"What do you know about him?" Dee fished.

"Nothing," Mack answered, which wasn't exactly true. She knew he was a detective and a danger to her sense of propriety.

"I'm going to Google him."

Mack squirmed uncomfortably. She was a huge proponent of privacy and hated the thought of Dee or anyone else cyberstalking someone who was looking to start over. Especially *him*. In their first brief encounter, Mack had seen glimpses of shadows in the detective's clear eyes. She'd bet her favorite Sig that Nick Benning had seen his share of ugliness. Maybe because she had been there, done that, and recognized the look.

"Dee, I don't think his prior personal life is any of your business."

"Anything I find will be a matter of public record. Besides, he's got this strong, silent, mysterious vibe going on. That is so sexy, don't you think?"

Mack could feel Delilah's eyes boring into her. Did Dee suspect that Mack harbored a hidden crush for her newest client? No, there was no way she could have. Mack's private thoughts were like Vegas: what happened there, stayed there.

"I suppose," Mack said non-committedly.

Dee looked at her as if she'd grown three heads, then her eyes grew wide. "Wait... you're not..." Dee lowered her voice to a hushed whisper, "... *you know*, are you?"

"No, I don't know. What the hell are you talking about?"

"You like girls, don't you?"

Mack stared at her in disbelief. Just because she was capable of controlling her baser impulses around every fit Tom, Dick, and Harry didn't mean she was walking the rainbow runway. "No, Dee. I'm not a lesbian."

"Are you sure? Because, it would be totally cool if you were."

"I'm not."

"I'm just saying…"

"I'm not gay."

"… because you *were* in the Marines, and you live with a gay guy."

"*I am not gay.* I have slept with — *do* sleep with — men, not women."

"And you *like* it?" Dee asked with wide eyes.

Mack clenched her teeth so hard she was in danger of snapping a few molars. "Yes."

"Oh. Okay." She still didn't look convinced, but Mack had had more than enough of the conversation. Thankfully, Jay glided in through the door in that moment, unwittingly saving Dee from wearing Mack's hands as a choker necklace.

"Hello, ladies," he sang. "How was little sis's first official week as a working girl?"

"Exhausting," Dee moaned dramatically, "but scenic. Did you give Tish my resume?"

Mack's mood instantly brightened. Tish was Jay's agent, a sharp, former runway model. Both Jay and Mack adored her; her passion for healthy, happy models over starved, miserable ones sent a lot of clients Mack's way. If Tish thought Dee had potential, Mack wouldn't feel obligated to keep Dee at *Seize*. It would be a win-win for everyone.

"I did," Jay told her. "Tish said to expect a call in a week or so, maybe earlier to come in for some test photos."

Exhaustion   temporarily   forgotten,   Dee

squealed, popping up off the couch and wrapping her arms around him. "Awesome, Jay. You are the best."

"I've been telling Mack that forever," he winked over Dee's shoulder.

Mack once again said a silent prayer of thanks for her housemate. He was the sweetest, most likable man she'd ever met. Not only was he being very cool about having Dee stay with them, he actually seemed to get along with her. That made the man a bona fide saint in Mack's eyes.

"Ussie!" Jay yelled suddenly, grabbing Mack around the shoulders and pulling her in close with him and Dee. Wearing a goofy smile, he stooped down, stuck out his tongue, made rock horns with the hand looped around her neck, and snapped a picture of the three of them on his latest and greatest i-gadget.

"Did you just call me a hussy?" Mack asked.

"No. I said *ussss*-eeee," he clarified, drawing the word out.

"What the hell is that?"

Dee gave Jay a sympathetic look and skipped off to get a shower. He turned the rectangular device around and showed Mack the picture. Jay, as always, looked stunning. Dee looked professionally Photoshopped. In contrast, Mack looked like she just rolled out of bed after a three-day bender. "It's like a *self*ie, but with all of *us*. Hence the term, *us*sie."

Mack snatched the phone from his hand and stared at him. "You're shitting me, right?"

He made a big X over his chest. "I shit you not. Haven't you ever taken one before? You know, with your unit or something?"

Brows creased in concentration, Mack thumbed the phone surface. "Sure. Every time we drove into a war-ravaged village we all gathered round the starving kids and snapped a pic for the folks back home."

"You don't have to be so sarcastic."

"Sarcasm is a sign of great intelligence."

He shook his head. "Do you have that embroidered on a pillow or something?"

"No." There was no way she was going to tell him that she did, in fact, have it printed on a T-shirt, a parting gift from her last team. Nor would she ever admit that they almost talked her into getting it tattooed on her rear end. Thank God she went with the Celtic cross and Trinity knot instead. "And don't dis sarcasm. It's not illegal or socially frowned upon like, say, beating the crap out of people."

He took a step back. "Sometimes you really scare me, Mack."

She grinned wickedly. "You should be scared."

"I'm terrified. Really. Now get that face over here so we can take a totally natural and unstaged picture since you just deleted the last one. You can post it on your Facebook profile so it looks like you have an actual life."

"I don't have a Facebook account."

He gaped at her. "You're killing me, Mack," he said, shaking his head. "I swear to God. Everyone over the age of twenty has, at the very minimum, accounts on Facebook, Twitter, and Instagram."

She blinked, her face blank. Chrissy, her honeymooning receptionist, handled all the social media stuff for *Seize*, and Mack had never really felt compelled to put her personal life out on the internet.

Jay muttered something unintelligible. She managed to pick up the words 'antisocial' and 'cavewoman' in there somewhere before he got that all-too-familiar look of determination on his face. "Baby girl, we are going to set you up. Where is your laptop?"

Like she was going to tell him. The man couldn't go fifteen minutes without texting, tweeting, snapping or Liking something. Mack didn't have the patience for sitting still for more than a minute at a time, let alone spending hours in front of a computer reading about other people's lives (although she did appreciate the occasional cute baby animal pics that Jay instant messaged her).

"I've got a better idea," her eyes suddenly lighting up.

He eyed her warily. "I'm seriously afraid to ask."

"Let's rusticate."

"Is that legal?"

"Fidiot. Rusticate means to unplug for a couple of days. Take a vacation from everything digital. No email, no computers, no cell phones." *No Delilah or tingle-inducing mysterious detectives.*

His expression was one of absolute horror. "You are insane."

"Am not. Come on, Jay. Next weekend. We'll hike the gorge, set up camp by the lake, cook over a fire, sleep under the stars. It'll be great."

"No way. I have a life, you know."

Mack sighed, deflated. "Yeah. Good point." She hadn't really expected him to go for it, but it had been worth a shot. She had yet to meet someone who shared her love of nature, of going off into the woods for a quick spiritual reboot instead of partying or hanging out. She spent every day surrounded by people, running a business, putting on a mask for everyone else. Was it so bad that she found solace in quiet time away from all that?

Jay looked at her with sympathy. "I'm sorry, Mack. I didn't mean it the way it sounded."

"Yeah, you did," she said, forcing a weak smile, "but it's okay. It is what it is."

"You are so freaking awesome!" he said, exasperated. "Why are you so afraid to let anyone see that?"

"*You* know," she said, rising up on her tiptoes to peck him on the cheek. "That's good enough for me."

"Mack, I know you don't like to hear this, but

__"

She reached up and put her finger on his lips. "Then don't say it, Jay, please. I'm heading over to *Seize*. Don't wait up."

He looked like he wanted to say more, but, smart man that he was, he didn't.

Chapter Nine

~ *Nick* ~

Nick sat in the parking lot of *Seize*, second-guessing his motives. He could say that he wanted to talk to Mack about possibly getting involved with her teen center, since many adult drug problems had their roots in those formative years. It would be the truth.

Or he could just admit he wanted to see Mack again.

He couldn't help it. Something about her had piqued his interest, kept her popping up in his thoughts despite everything else he had going on.

Complicated, that's what she was. Hard to read. Friendly, but distant. Confident, yet wary. Sexy, yet down-to-earth. Even more intriguing: beneath all that beauty and strength, was a woman with a lot of secrets, he'd bet his shield on it.

Nick grabbed his workout bag out of the back seat and locked up his car. Still questioning the wisdom of his actions, Nick couldn't deny the frisson of pleasure he felt at the sight of Mack at the front desk, eyes narrowed, cheeks colored. Just like the first time he'd seen her, her shoulders were tense and she was muttering to herself.

"Fucking unbelievable. I mean, how hard is it? Answer the phone. Press a few keys..."

Sensing his presence, Mack cut off her barely audible tirade and glanced up. Her eyes flashed with heat, sparking his own before her expression went oddly neutral. "Detective Benning."

"Nick," he corrected, trying to hide his grin. "Problems?"

"Nothing I can't handle."

"I don't doubt it. Do you have a few minutes? There's something I'd like to speak with you about."

She studied him carefully, her guard back in place. "Sure. Hey Toni, can you cover the front desk for a few?"

An attractive woman nodded and waved goodbye to a group of middle-aged women in track suits and yoga pants on their way out. "Good job, ladies. Rest up. Next time we're going to incorporate some piloxing into our routine." She laughed at the resulting groans and stepped over, offering him a friendly smile. "New guy, right?"

"Right."

"Toni, Nick Benning. Nick, Toni Carminetti, body sculptor extraordinaire."

The woman's eyes twinkled. "Always glad to see a member of Covendale's finest at *Seize*." She turned to the computer, her brows drawing together at whatever she saw on the screen. "Oh my. What happened there?"

"*Dee* happened," Mack said on an exhale. "Do me a favor, will you? When Bill's done with his workout, can you ask him to take a look at this?"

"On it, boss."

"Thanks, Toni." She waved to Nick, inviting him to follow her into her office. "So... what did you want to talk to me about? Are you having any problems or issues?"

The leggy blonde who'd been skulking around came to mind, but he kept his mouth shut. "Just the opposite, actually. This place is great."

"Glad to hear it," Mack said. Was he imagining it, or did she seem relieved?

"I wanted to speak with you about this safe zone you've created for teens."

Her eyes opened wide. "Oh?"

"It's great that you give them a place to go, positive things to do."

"Thanks."

"You're welcome. I'd like to help."

"What did you have in mind?"

Wholly inappropriate ideas popped into his mind, ideas that had nothing whatsoever to do with the teen program and everything to do with the woman asking. He confined his response to the topic at hand. "Adolescence is a turbulent time for kids. It's when they're at their most vulnerable. They're still trying to figure everything out and not all of them have someone to help them with the answers. I've found that getting involved at this stage builds a positive relationship between kids and law enforcement and encourages trust and open communication."

Her shoulders tensed and the corners of her mouth dipped southward. "You want to use my kids for information?"

"What? No!" He shook his head vehemently. "I want them to know they have someone they can go to when they have questions or problems. This is a rough age for them, Mack. Peer pressure, lots of changes."

"And you think they're going to open up to a cop?" she asked doubtfully.

"A cop, no. But someone they know? Someone they can trust? Yes, maybe. Hopefully."

The tense lines on her face softened. "They're good kids, Detective."

"I don't doubt it. And I'd like to keep it that way."

Mack sat back, her expression thoughtful, but her eyes were as sharp as ever. At that moment, they were focused on him, gauging his sincerity. "This is important to you?"

He met her gaze with one of his own. "Very."

"Why?"

"Excuse me?"

"*Why* is it so important to you?"

He carefully weighed his answer. There were a lot of reasons he could give her, but she wanted truth. She really cared about these kids, he realized, his respect for her continuing to grow with each tick of the clock.

"Because I've chosen to make Covendale my home. Because I've seen enough young lives ruined by drugs, alcohol, and violence. Because I believe I can make a difference, not just on the clock, but off of it as well."

"This is about more than the job for you," she said softly.

She had no idea. "Yes. Many years ago, I... lost someone important to me."

He waited, holding her gaze. Eventually she nodded. "All right, Detective. How about we do something on a trial basis and see how it goes?"

"Perfect. I can come by a couple of times a week, hang out, get to know them."

Her lips quirked, as if she found the idea amusing. "They're teens and pre-teens. They're naturally suspicious of anyone over twenty-one."

"Then I guess I'll just have to convince them — and you — to trust me."

Chapter Ten

~ *Mack* ~

Mack hung back, watching the detective as he executed a jump shot. *Poetry in motion*, she thought, quietly enjoying the way he moved, the ripple of muscles from his broad shoulders all the way down to his impressive quads and well-toned calves.

He'd coaxed some of the boys into a pick-up game, taunting them good-naturedly about age and experience trumping youth and agility. The teens were wary but seemed to be responding well to him.

She wasn't entirely surprised. Nick Benning was a very lickable – uh, *likeable* – guy.

He had a friendly, approachable manner, but came across as strong and capable too. When Jesse, one of the older teens, challenged him with some attitude, Nick had firmly established himself as the one in charge without embarrassing the kid. That took some skill, and Mack was dutifully impressed.

Not for the first time, she wondered what Nick's deal was. He projected an air of quiet, capable authority that she found as attractive as his athletic physique, but there was something more there, too. Something in his eyes that suggested he'd seen his share of tragedy, something that attested to a deeper appreciation for life than most. That kind of thing left an intangible mark. She'd seen it plenty of times in her fellow Marines and in those who had faced a big challenge and come out on the other side, intact but essentially changed.

Mack supposed it was only to be expected. Nick was a cop, and if he'd worked in a big city like Chicago, he must have seen his share of bad things. Or maybe it had something to do with the reference he'd made to losing someone.

Though she'd been tempted, Mack refused to stoop to Dee's level of Googling him. Whatever it was that had marked him, it was his business and none of hers.

Unless, for some unfathomable reason, he decided to share it with her.

And why, a little voice deep in her psyche wanted to know, *would he ever want to do that?*

The obvious answer: he wouldn't.

Mack gave herself a mental shake, reminding herself that Nick was a client. Her interest had to remain strictly professional. Which also meant she probably shouldn't be gawking at him as she was.

Satisfied that Nick had things under control, she wrangled her sudden thirst and quietly slipped away. As nice as the view had been, she had other things to take care of. Like trying to prevent a harassment suit because her man-hungry stepsister couldn't keep her hands to herself.

"Dee!" she barked, rounding the corner to see her stepsister about to invade the personal space of Harrison Kennedy, one of Mack's favorite people. The chief loan officer at Covendale Fidelity Bank and Trust, he'd been instrumental in helping her turn *Seize* from a dream into a reality. As a result, he had a lifetime free membership and her infinite gratitude.

Harrison sent her a thankful look and made a smooth getaway. Dee, on the other hand, scowled and hissed, "Now what? God, Mack, you are such a cock block!"

Mack put a pin in the "boundaries" lecture she was going to give Dee — again — to correct her. "Cock block is something guys do."

Dee sniffed. "He's got a cock, doesn't he? And you just blocked me from getting to it."

Mack grabbed Dee's arm and pulled her into an empty room. "Harrison Kennedy is a pillar of this community and one hell of a good guy. He's also very married."

"So?"

"Back off, Dee. Last warning."

"Fine," Dee huffed. "But you know, some guys

actually like a little attention. You might try it sometime."

Mack ignored the jibe and went down to one of the practice rooms and took out some of her frustration on one of the mannequins they used for MMA classes. She would never admit it, but Dee had a point. Most people, men and women included, liked to feel attractive and desired once in a while. Herself included.

Mack pulled on a pair of fingerless, padded gloves and warmed up with a couple of stretches and simple katas. The thing was, Mack was shit at that kind of thing. Honest praise and encouragement, sure — she doled that out like a champ. But flirting? Batting her eyelashes and spewing sexual innuendo? Stuff that seemed to come naturally for most women just wasn't in her wheelhouse.

Not everyone was cast from the same mold. So she wasn't a femme fatale, so what? Being selective, not settling for just any handsome face or hot body — there was nothing wrong with that, no matter what Dee or anyone else thought. The few, completely unremarkable encounters she'd had convinced her that she was better off waiting for someone who made her heart beat faster just by looking at her.

Like Nick Benning, for example.

She let out a fierce Kiai, a short shout-out when performing an attacking move, pivoting on her leg and kicking the bag hard. Letting her body take control, Mack lost herself in a series of movements, a dance of her own creation, incorporating a combination of offensive and defensive movements designed to focus the mind and tax her body. By the time she was finished, her body was covered in sweat and her muscles were screaming, but her head was clearer.

Maybe she was overreacting. Projecting her own, deeply-buried sense of inadequacy out on Dee. Most of the guys *did* seem to enjoy Dee's attention. There hadn't been a single registered complaint, but was that because they really didn't mind or because they thought Mack would take it personally? She'd just have to stay on top of it and make sure things didn't get out of hand.

She turned and reached for a towel, only then realizing that a small crowd had gathered. Carl was there, grinning like an idiot. A former special ops man who had spent more than a dozen years deep in the Middle East, he had taken her rudimentary MMA skills to the next level and beyond.

"You okay there, boss? That was a hell of a show."

"Sorry about that," she said quietly as Carl's class filed in. "I should have checked the schedule."

"No problem," he said, his eyes glistening. "Couldn't ask for a better promo."

She laughed, inclining her head toward the students. "Then I'm glad to help."

"Seriously, Mack. Everything okay?"

"Yeah, fine. Just working off a bit of Dee-inspired angst."

He nodded knowingly. "Gotcha. In that case, a few simple katas aren't going to cut it. Want to stick around and help me with the self-defense lesson?"

Help Carl with his class or go back to the front desk and deal with Dee? It was a no-brainer. "Do I get to kick your ass?"

"You could try."

"Then you're on."

Chapter Eleven

~ *Nick* ~

It didn't take long for Nick to settle into a comfortable routine. He had yet to get in touch with Liz, but otherwise, things were coming along nicely. He'd moved into the Cape Cod and was appreciating the peace, quiet, and space. He took joy in the simple pleasures of mowing the lawn and trimming the bushes, things he hadn't been able to do while living in an apartment or motel.

The job was going well, too. Nick had a lot of respect for Sam Brown and liked (most of) the people he worked with. Unlike Emerson, they didn't seem to harbor any underlying animosity. A few of the uniforms cast hairy eyeballs his way occasionally, but since he'd also seen those same cops cozying up to Emerson, it wasn't unexpected.

He'd already closed one of the four cases he'd been assigned and he'd set up a meeting with the local school board about ramping up their drug and alcohol awareness and resistance program in the fall. He spent a fair share of his limited free time at *Seize*, working out, building a rapport with the kids… and seeking out the elusive and enigmatic woman who'd unknowingly gotten under his skin.

"Come on, Mack. Admit it. I won." Nick grinned down at her, holding the towel high in the air, just out of her reach. It wasn't difficult since he was nearly a foot taller than her and had a much longer wingspan. Yeah, he knew he was pressing her buttons, but he couldn't help it. It was as if a little devil was sitting on his shoulder, goading him into tugging her pigtails, so to speak.

It hadn't taken much effort to learn her routine, and despite telling himself he was playing with fire, he had made a point of crossing paths with her at least once a day. He couldn't say why, exactly, except that he wanted to.

He liked her. Liked her sass. Her confidence. The way she seemed determined not to encourage him even though her pupils dilated whenever he managed to get near her. Clearly, she had no idea that by doing so, she was only piquing his interest.

Nick liked a challenge and, since his job wasn't exactly a nine-to-five, he often appeared at different times throughout the day, keeping her on her toes. She never knew when to expect him, which meant it was more difficult for her to avoid him.

She put her hands on her hips and glared up at him with a look that would have made a lesser man cower. "I bet you have sisters you like to torment, don't you?"

"Just one." He grinned wider, more aroused than intimidated by her scowl. "But she's bigger than you."

Mack snorted. When he'd found her, she was just finishing up ten miles on the treadmill's digitally simulated course. He didn't know what made him snatch the workout towel out of her grasp before she could wipe away the sheen of perspiration; it was just an impulse he hadn't tried hard to resist. With her skin flushed from her run and glistening like that, she looked sexy as hell.

"You are such an adultolescent."

He narrowed his eyes at her. "What did you just call me?"

"An adultolescent." She rolled her eyes. Even that was attractive when Mack did it. "A person who has physically matured to adulthood, yet still behaves like an adolescent."

"You made that up." Even if it did fit the situation remarkably well.

"Did not. Google it."

He didn't, because he already knew by the confident gleam in her eye that he would find it and the definition would be exactly what she said it was, probably word for word. She was annoyingly knowledgeable that way, he'd discovered after a few well-timed, "coincidental" run-ins and some discreet investigation. His background in profiling didn't hurt, either.

"How am I an adulto-whatever-you-said?"

"Adulto*lescent*," she corrected, taking advantage of his momentary loss of focus to make an impressive vertical leap and snatch the towel from his hands. "You're a six-foot-two cop resorting to juvenile taunting just because you managed to beat me in a video game created for six-year-olds."

He grinned widely at the reminder. Earlier, he'd tracked her to the center's lounge, where she had been talking to a few of the pre-teens about upcoming sports try-outs. Somehow, he had managed to goad her into playing a video game with him (he may have shamelessly enlisted the support of the kids). Of course, she had no way of knowing that in Chicago, he'd worked with kids who ate, slept, and breathed the stuff. As a result, he had systematically handed Mack her ass in a best-of-three series of Mario Kart.

"Yeah, well you're a sore loser," he teased. "Do you know what that is, or should I Google that for you?

"I am not a sore loser," she sniffed, lifting her chin. "I openly admit to sucking at video games. Best me at a real contest."

His masculine interest surged. This was the first time she had suggested any interaction beyond their "coincidental" crossing of paths. It could be just the opening he'd been hoping for. "Such as?"

She scrunched up her nose as she thought about it. It was so damn cute. "Archery."

"Who are you, Katniss Everdeen?" he quipped.

She smirked. "Can't handle pointy sticks. Got it. What about hand-to-hand combat?"

He scoffed, though the lower half of his

anatomy found the idea of getting up close and personal quite appealing. "Please. I've had dogs bigger than you."

"Scared?" she taunted.

He snorted, but yeah, he was scared, all right. Scared of what it was about this woman that kept drawing him in. Scared of the dreams that kick-ass, sexy body of hers inspired. The most remarkable thing was, he didn't think she had any idea she was doing it.

The way she was pointedly looking him up and down with that scheming, predatory gleam in her eyes wasn't doing much to help matters, either. If she kept looking at him like that, he was going to get an embarrassing tent in his shorts like the adolescent she'd just accused him of being.

"Hey, you're a cop. You've got a gun, right?"

"It's kind of required so, yeah," he said instantly wary.

"Can you shoot it?"

He crossed his arms over his chest and widened his stance. "Of course I can."

"Perfect. O'Malley's Firing Range. Know it?"

He had passed it a few times, knew that guys on the force went there to keep their skills sharp. The place hadn't been around ten years ago, but he'd been to enough just like it.

"You're serious?"

"Deadly."

"Okay," he said, drawing the word out slowly. "But it's only fair I warn you that I hold the record for marksmanship at the academy."

She shrugged, completely unimpressed. That probably shouldn't have been as arousing as it was. "Talk is cheap, Detective."

"Nick," he corrected automatically. "You're on, Mack. Winner gets… what?"

Her eyes lost focus for a minute as she considered his question. "I kick your butt, you have to take a Zumba class."

His brows knitted together. "And if I win?"

Mack snorted in laughter, doubling over and putting her hands on her knees. "Yeah, right, okay. Sorry, give me a minute…"

His eyes narrowed. "You don't think I can beat you?"

"Hell, no," she said, still laughing as she wiped the tears from her eyes.

"Fine. I'll tell you what, smart ass. I agree to your terms, but if I win, *you* take a Zumba class, *and* you do it in your underwear."

Mack stopped laughing. "Seriously?"

He smirked. "Put up or shut up, Mack."

Chapter Twelve

~ *Mack* ~

Mack only hesitated for a moment before agreeing to his terms. First, as good as he claimed to be, she was damn sure she wasn't going to lose. He wasn't the only one at the top of his class. And even if she *did* lose, most of her underwear consisted of boy shorts and full coverage, minimizing sports bras anyway, not the lacy thongs and push-up bras he was probably envisioning. *Ha!*

She stuck out her hand. "Deal. I've got a standing reservation booked at the range every Tuesday, six o'clock. Oh, and would you look at that? Today just happens to be Tuesday."

He grinned, enveloping her small hand with his much larger one. She tried not to jolt at the sudden and unexpected rush of energy that flowed between them, intensifying the tingles already present because of his close proximity.

"I'm there," he told her. "But don't you want to

insist that if I lose I have to take the class in *my* underwear?"

Mack pictured him in a tight pair of boxer briefs, hugging his nice ass and with her luck, a nicely wrapped package as well. No way in hell she wanted to flaunt that in front of a class of women high on endorphins. Not because she was jealous (that sudden spike of aggression she felt was definitely *not* jealousy) but because the good detective wouldn't stand a chance in a class of she-wolves.

"No, Detective," she told him with a wicked smile. "I was thinking more along the line of cheetah-print spandex..."

Absolute horror flashed briefly in his eyes before being replaced by smug confidence. He actually believed he could win. It was cute.

Mack took her leave, feeling rather pleased with herself. Was this what flirting felt like? A sense of buoyancy and anticipation for what might come next?

No, she corrected herself. This wasn't a *date*, not in the true sense of the word. It was more like a friendly competition for bragging rights. Dates didn't take place at firing ranges. When a couple when out on a *date*-date, dinner or a movie or something that didn't include the use of firearms was usually involved.

But maybe, just maybe, after she kicked his ass, she'd suggest a stop at Ground Zero for a coffee or something... *if* he wasn't a sore loser.

The rest of the afternoon dragged by. Despite

her efforts not to read too much into their wager, she was looking forward to seeing him. Lusty secret fantasies aside, he seemed like a genuinely nice guy.

After work, she rushed home, wolfed down a quick salad, then grabbed a shower and put on her best pair of jeans (the ones that made her ass look great), form-fitting tank, and a short-sleeved cotton overshirt (which she kept unbuttoned). The outfit wouldn't win her any commendations by the fashion police, but it had the benefit of flattering her figure while remaining within her narrow zone of comfort.

Not that she was trying to impress anyone. Much.

She pulled into O'Malley's fifteen minutes early and scanned the vehicles already there. She had no idea what Nick drove, but since she recognized every car in the lot, she knew he hadn't yet arrived. That was good. It would give her a few extra minutes to warm up.

She greeted the regulars, ignoring their questioning looks as they took in her nicer-than-normal appearance, and pulled out her favorite handgun, a P320 X-Five Full-Size.

What kind of gun did Nick prefer, she wondered? Was he a Glock man? A .45 ACP? 9mm? A man's weapon of choice said a lot about him. She hoped he wasn't the flashy, look-at-my-big-gun type. They were the ones usually overcompensating.

She didn't think Nick was overcompensating.

At 6:30 pm, Mack took a deep breath, then held it, her body as still as a marble statue. She fired off another round at the target, alternating kill shots to the head and chest. She wasn't angry, and she wasn't disappointed. Because if she *was* either of those things, then it would mean that she had, on some level, actually been expecting him to show.

Which would have been really, really stupid.

"Remind me not to piss you off," Chaz grinned when she removed the ear protectors and handed them back to him. Mack smiled back at the sixty-something retired Ranger who ran the place. "Probably a good idea."

"Do I know him?"

"Who?"

He shifted the ever-present cinnamon toothpick to the other side of his mouth with a well-practiced movement. "Whoever's got you shooting like that. Shit, Mack. You'd make one hell of a sniper, you know that?"

She grinned and shook her head as she signed the spent targets. "You've got it all wrong, Chaz. There's not a man alive with a pair of balls big enough to think he can handle me."

He laughed. "If only I was thirty years younger, Mack, you wouldn't be able to run far or fast enough." He shook his head. "Don't know what's wrong with these guys today. Can't handle a real woman."

A small pang shot across her chest. He had no idea how much his words meant, even if he was just saying them to be kind. Kindness for kindness' sake was just so rare.

"You know it," she said, smiling through the sudden, unwelcome wash of melancholy. "I'll be back next week, yeah?"

"Hey, Mack," he called as she was about to head out the door. "Mind if I hang a couple of these up? Show these posers how it's done?"

Mack looked at the spent targets he held in his hand, allowing herself a tiny ribbon of pride. "Sure. Knock yourself out."

Chapter Thirteen

~ *Nick* ~

"That's him," Jesse Walker said quietly from the back of the car. Jesse's mother, sitting next to her son, nodded in affirmation.

From their position half a block down from Jesse's house, they had a clear view of the big, bearded man as he got off his bike and made a beeline for the front door. Jesse Walker, Sr. had just been released from prison after serving time for a multitude of crimes and, despite a restraining order, had decided to make their house the second stop on his freedom tour. The first had been the clubhouse of the outlaw motorcycle club he belonged to.

The man moved slowly but with definite purpose, staggering once or twice as he made his way up the walk. If the bulges in his jacket were any indication, the guy was packing, adding yet another item to the fast-growing list of things parolees were not supposed to have or do.

"Okay. Sit tight and stay here. Everything is going to be okay."

Jesse nodded and put his arm around his trembling mother. Nick spoke quietly into his phone, then exited his vehicle and started walking toward the house. Several police cars pulled up at the same time, surrounding the man. Jesse Senior tried to run, but he was taken down quickly and subdued.

Less than forty-eight hours after being released, he was headed right back to prison. This time, Nick was going to make sure he stayed there for a very long time.

Nick drove Jesse and his mother to the station where they filled out a formal report, then gave them a ride home. He declined an offer of dinner but thanked them for offering. As he walked back to his car, Jesse followed.

"Hey, Nick. Uh, thanks."

Nick took the hand the teen extended and looked directly into the boy's eyes. "You're welcome. You did the right thing in calling me, Jesse."

Jesse nodded and turned to go back into the house, then paused. "Listen, if you're serious about wanting to do something…"

"I am."

"There's this guy that's been coming around every couple days. Name's Zeke. He's a prospect at my old man's MC, and word is he's taken over distribution. But you didn't hear that from me."

"Hear what?" Nick asked. The kid's eyes

flashed with approval.

Nick got back into his car, feeling pretty good about the way things had turned out. What could have been a bad situation all around had been resolved quietly and peacefully. Jesse Senior was on his way back to prison, and Jesse and his mom were safe.

The fact that Jesse had called him meant that Nick was making progress in building a sense of trust with the teens at the center and in the community. An added bonus: now he had a solid lead on who was bringing the drugs into the area and targeting kids.

To top it all off, he was going to finish out the day by meeting up with Mack.

Nick looked at the dashboard display and groaned. It was much later than he'd thought.

With no time to go back to his place and change, Nick made his way across town, thankful the traffic wasn't too bad. By the time he pulled into O'Malley's, the clock read seven. Still in his suit and tie, Nick jogged across the lot, hoping he hadn't missed her.

An older guy with a buzz cut looked up from his ammo supply catalog, pinning Nick with cold, clear light blue eyes. He had military written all over him. If Nick had to guess, he'd say special forces. "Can I help you?"

"Yeah, I'm supposed to meet someone here. Is Mack still around?"

The guy's eyes narrowed. "Who wants to know?"

"Nick. Nick Benning."

Nick offered a friendly smile, but it wasn't returned. Those blue eyes assessed him, much the way Mack's had the first time he'd seen her. "You look like a cop."

"Detective, actually."

"Ah. You're the new guy."

Nick nodded. He found it was easier to go with that than explain that he'd grown up in Covendale, moved away, and decided to return to his roots.

The older guy stared at him for a few minutes, absently chewing a toothpick. Then he smirked and chuckled, leaving Nick feeling as if he had just missed something important. "Mack's been and gone." He jerked his thumb to the targets now proudly displayed behind him.

Nick saw Mack's name scribbled at the bottom and couldn't help but be impressed. Maybe it was a good thing he'd been held up; otherwise, he might be shaking his ass in spandex.

"She's good, huh?"

"Mack? She's the best." The warning was clear in the older man's tone. Those icy blue eyes lit on him like a laser. Nick had the distinct impression the guy wasn't just talking about her high-accuracy shooting.

Nick refused to cower under the guy's gaze and met it with one of his own. "I don't suppose you'd know where I could find her?"

"You're a detective. You figure it out."

"Right. Thanks."

Nick turned to leave, feeling the guy's gaze on

his back. Clearly, the guy felt protective of Mack, and that, Nick could respect. He was more concerned with what *Mack* thought when he hadn't shown. Did she think he'd stood her up? Or, knowing he was a cop, had she given him the benefit of the doubt?

He slid into the driver's seat and sighed. He was more than a little rusty at this kind of thing. For ten years, the job had always come first. It had been a long time since he'd been interested enough to wonder about things like impressions and misunderstandings on a personal level. However, he did remember enough to realize he owed Mack an explanation, and sooner rather than later. With any luck, she might be willing to meet him for a quick bite or maybe some coffee.

But first, he had to get her number.

He pointed the car toward *Seize*. Mack wasn't there, but Carl was. When Nick explained the situation, Carl called out to a sculpted blonde guy who was just emerging from the weight room area.

"Hey Jay, come here for a minute, will you?"

"What's up?"

"Nick here is asking how to contact Mack."

The guy called Jay turned to Nick. "Detective Benning, right? Nice to meet you. I'm Jay, Mack's housemate. Is there a problem?"

Mack's housemate? This guy lived with Mack? He had male model written all over him, from his artfully tousled hair and perfect white teeth to his cut, fit physique. A wave of something dark and possessive tried to rise up, but Nick pushed it down.

"I was supposed to meet up with Mack, but I got held up at work and missed her."

Jay narrowed his eyes. "You had a date with Mack?"

"Is that a problem?"

The words came out with an edge he hadn't been able to fully suppress. Rather than take offense, a smile curved Jay's lips. "No worries, Detective. Mack and I are many things to each other, but lovers isn't one of them."

Relief coursed through him. "I was supposed to meet Mack at O'Malley's."

"Mixing Mack *and* firearms? You are a brave man."

"Well, Nick, I am going to do you a solid." Jay peeled off a sticky note from a stack on the desk and scribbled a number. "This is Mack's personal cell, but if you tell her you got it from me, I'll deny it."

"Deal. Thanks."

"Oh, and Detective? Mack and I might not be involved that way, but she *is* my closest and dearest friend. I care about her very much."

Jay pinned him with a hard look, and Nick took it for what it was: a warning. "Understood."

Chapter Fourteen

~ *Mack* ~

Nick: *Sorry I missed you.*

Wearing another "borrowed" pair of Jay's boxers and an oversized *Seize* T, Mack sat cross-legged on her bed and re-read the text, wondering how Nick got her cell number. Then she remembered what he did for a living and felt stupid. It would be child's play for a detective to find her mobile number.

Mack briefly considered blowing him off, then realized that would make it seem like she was bothered by the fact that he'd failed to show. She wasn't. Not at all. Why would she be?

Mack: *No problem.*

Nick: *Something came up at work.*

She'd figured as much. It was either that or Nick had deliberately blown her off, and he didn't seem like the type to do that. The situation did provide her with a much-needed dose of reality, however. Nick's job was a priority, which she understood perfectly.

Mack: *It happens.*

Nick: *Too late to grab a coffee?*

Mack's thumb hovered over the screen. Was he serious or just being polite? Either way, it didn't really matter. The evening had proven that she was in over her head when it came to Nick Benning. She could tell herself they could just be friends, but the tingles and sense of anticipation she felt whenever she was around him proved otherwise. Until she got control over that, avoidance was her best option.

Mack: *Yes, sorry.*

Nick: *Raincheck?*

Mack: *Sure.* She tapped out the response, confident she wouldn't have to make good on it. Something else would come up. She'd make sure of it.

Nick: *What are you doing now?*

Mack stared at the screen, surprised. He wanted to know what she was doing? At least he didn't ask her what she was wearing.

She snorted, then mentally chastised herself. He was *not* interested in her. He was just a nice guy who felt bad about standing her up and was trying to make amends with light, topical conversation. Obviously, he didn't realize that it wasn't necessary, because show or no-show, it meant nothing more than something to do.

And because it meant nothing, she answered him honestly.

Mack: *Getting ready for bed.*

Nick: *Kind of early for that, isn't it?*

Mack: *It's been a long day and I have to get up early.*

Minutes ticked by while she chewed her lip and waited for a response. Had he picked up on her subtle clues? Or was he, at that very moment, shrugging out of his work clothes into something more comfortable? Making himself something to eat? Images of Nick, shirtless in his kitchen, came to mind. Was he a frozen entrée kind of guy, or did he like to cook?

Her phone dinged with an incoming message, breaking her away from that appealing visual.

Nick: *Okay. Goodnight, Mack.*

Well, that was easy, she thought. Not even a half-hearted attempt to keep her talking. She was glad she'd had the foresight not to take things too seriously, because if she had gotten her hopes up, they'd be crashing and burning with disappointment for a second time that evening.

Mack: *Goodnight, Detective.*

Mack punched her pillow and tried to put Nick Benning out of her thoughts. It didn't work. Each time she closed her eyes, images of his mischievous smile and laughing eyes kept popping up.

Eventually, she gave up and got up, grabbing her laptop in the hopes of distracting herself with work. By midnight, she'd completed the class schedules through the end of the quarter. By one, she'd outlined a new combined strength/cardio program geared toward busy moms. At two, she finally put the computer away and fell into a restless, exhausted sleep.

When her alarm went off, she dragged her ass out of bed and made an extra-strong pot of coffee.

"Mack!" Dee called from the second floor. Mack groaned. She was in no mood to deal with Delilah. She ignored the summons and sipped her coffee.

"Now, Mack!" Dee whined from the second floor. "Come here *right now*. It's urgent."

Mack closed her eyes and prayed for patience. Dee's idea of "urgent" was probably a chip in her gel manicure or, God forbid, a blemish. After a restless night, all Mack wanted to do was have a peaceful cup of coffee on the porch before she went in to work. Was that too much to ask?

Gulping down the last of the brew, she took a deep breath and steeled herself for what she would find. She was glad she'd taken those extra moments when she found Dee standing naked in the guest bathroom wearing nothing but a scowl and shoving an iPhone toward Mack.

"Take a picture right now while I've got my morning-skinny going."

Ah, yes. That magical time after a morning trip to the bathroom and before eating breakfast, when Dee was at her absolute least weight of the day.

"Got your weigh-in today?" Mack guessed. Jay had gotten her in for an initial interview with the modeling agency. As part of that, Delilah was required to undergo a series of check-ins where she was weighed and measured, analyzed for percentage of body fat, and assessed for overall health.

Following standard locker room protocol, Mack tried not to look directly at Dee. Instead, her eyes fell on the dizzying assortment of creams, lotions, and gels covering nearly every surface. Just thinking about the effort involved in using all that stuff made her tired. If that was what it took to be beautiful, Mack was quite content to stick with her plain-Jane regimen.

"Yes. And I am *freaking out*! I gained half a pound this week!"

Mack's eyes moved to the pile of satin thongs and matching push-up bras littering the floor. She'd need to sew about a dozen or so of those tiny patches together to cover her bits. It seemed kind of pointless really. A few postage stamps would work just as well and were a hell of a lot cheaper.

"Wow. A whole half-pound. Should we go tent shopping?"

"Don't be mean."

"It's who I am."

"Mack, this is serious! What if I don't get the modeling contract?"

Mack knew Tish well enough to know that a half pound one way or the other certainly wasn't going to make a difference, but she didn't bother to say so. Dee was having a moment and wouldn't listen anyway. Besides, Mack really wasn't in the mood to blow sunshine up her ass.

"So what if you don't?"

"What else would I do?"

Well, that was a good question. Dee really

wasn't qualified for anything, and her princess mentally wouldn't permit any sort of menial labor. "You have a job at *Seize*," Mack reminded her, tacking a silent *for now* onto the end. After her father returned and took Dee off her hands, Mack really couldn't care less what she did.

Delilah actually shuddered, a full-bodied event that rippled from the top of her bleached hair to the tips of her French pedicure. "Man candy aside, you can't be serious. Doing a Zumba class is hard, Mack. And I *perspire*." She said the word like sweating was a bad thing.

"It is a fitness center, Dee. People go there to work out and yes, they sweat in the process. It's a good thing."

"It's disgusting. A good cleanse a couple of times a month and daily purges accomplish the same thing and require much less effort. Oh, Mack. What am I going to do?"

Mack clenched her teeth together and tried to digest the fact that in Dee's mind, she hadn't said or done anything offensive. Was there a more self-absorbed person on the planet?

"Ugh! I never should have had that slice of bread yesterday. Carbs are so evil," Dee was muttering.

Mack knew better. "Not all carbs are evil, Delilah," she said on an exhale.

"Well, just look at you, Mack."

For the briefest of moments, Mack froze. She should have been used to it, but it still hurt. Every freaking time.

"Yeah, look at me." Try as she might to stop it, some of the pain came through her voice.

Delilah huffed, as if *she* were the one insulted. "God, Mack. You make everything about you. I didn't mean it like that."

Yeah, she did. Because Dee wasn't happy unless everyone else felt like crap. It wasn't enough that she was every man's fantasy; she wanted to be every woman's envy, too.

Mack turned away from the bathroom and started walking down the steps before she said what she really thought.

"Hey. Where are you going? What about my picture?"

Fuck your picture. "Take it yourself," Mack shot back. "I'm late."

Chapter Fifteen

~ Nick ~

The morning after their non-meet, Nick got up extra early with a plan in mind. He hit up Ground Zero and bought two coffees with the intention of giving one to Mack as a peace offering. With any luck, they could share a few moments together before he went into work. Not only did he want to apologize in person, but he also wanted to explain *why* he'd been late. Jesse's call was a direct result of his involvement with the teen program, and since Mack had been instrumental in making that happen, he wanted her to feel good about that.

Mack wasn't manning the front desk when he entered; a fresh-faced young woman sporting a healthy tan was. He didn't need his shield to deduce that she was the eloping receptionist. Her radiant glow said it all.

"Hi! I'm Chrissy. Welcome to *Seize*!" She

spoke quickly and with a natural ebullience.

"Good morning. Is—" He didn't get the chance to ask if Mack was around before she barreled forward.

"You're Nick Benning, aren't you? I saw your file. Your two-week trial is just about up. How do you like it so far? You love it, right?"

"Yes, it's—"

"It's awesome, I know!" She grinned, showcasing a set of deep-set dimples. "Ooo, is that from Ground Zero? They have the *best* coffee. I stopped on my way in this morning and got their Morning Motivator with an extra turbo shot. It's a real eye opener!"

No kidding, he thought, fighting the urge to chuckle. "Is Mack around?"

She looked from his face to the cup and back to his face, her eyes acquiring a knowing (and approving) gleam as realization dawned. "She was just here a minute ago. Want me to page her?"

"No, that won't be necessary." He grabbed a felt pen from the desk and wrote "Do over?" on the side of the heavy paper cup, then handed it to the young woman. "If you see that she gets this, I'd appreciate it."

Chrissy looked at what he'd written, her smile growing to epic proportions. "I will."

Leaving a "gift" for Mack at the front desk was a risky move, but the starry-eyed newlywed receptionist might provide the extra nudge that would get Mack to agree to give him another chance.

...Or it could backfire in a major way.

Regardless, Nick's instincts told him he'd have to step up his game if he wanted to get to know the enigmatic owner better, and he did, so...

Sipping his coffee (which was pretty damn amazing), he drove over to the station. He'd already started compiling dossiers on members of the Necromancers MC, but he didn't recall coming across any information on a "Zeke". Then again, most of the information was from a few years earlier and sketchy at best. When he questioned Kent Emerson about it, Emerson shrugged and said there was no need because the club kept a low profile.

Nick wasn't sure if that mindset was rooted in naivete, ignorance, or just plain laziness. Regardless, his opinion of Emerson dropped another notch. If the guy put as much time and effort into his work as he did into chasing tail, he would have recognized the threat the Necromancers posed.

Of course, it helped when one knew what to look for. With a few targeted searches, Nick was able to gather enough information to suggest the club was more than an isolated, small-town operation. Within a couple hours, Nick had compiled a list of possible connections to some big names, names that he knew from his stint in

Chicago and before that, Seattle.

He shared some of what he found with the chief, who agreed that the club warranted a closer look. Before he left, Sam commended him on bringing about a peaceful resolution to the Jesse Walker situation.

"That could have been a real shit show," Sam told him candidly. "Jesse's been trouble for as long as I can remember," adding, "I'm glad to hear his son is taking a different path."

Nick was, too.

After putting out some calls, Nick was surprised to see how much time had passed. Once he started digging, he often lost track of time. He stood up and stretched, wincing when his joints protested with audible pops. While he was waiting to hear back from his contacts, he figured it was as good a time as any to check in with the kids and squeeze in a quick workout. And this time, he would make sure his path crossed with Mack's.

The leggy blonde — Delilah — was at the reception desk when he entered. Nick had seen her around *Seize* several times; she seemed to gravitate toward areas with a heavy concentration of men. He tried to avoid her whenever possible, but like the proverbial bad penny, she kept showing up.

Today she was wearing her usual scowl, paying more attention to her phone than the customers coming and going. He thought he'd be able to slip by unnoticed, but in a classic case of bad timing, she looked up as he was making his way across the lobby.

"Detective!" she purred. She rose from the chair in a move of smooth, feminine grace. Her eyes burned with predatory interest as she leaned over the desk, showcasing her low-cut, skin-tight top. "It's *so* nice to see you again."

'Nice' wasn't the word he would choose. She reminded him too much of Eve Sanderson. Not just in physical appearance, but in behavior as well. She had the same calculating gleam and used her feminine assets to get what she wanted.

Based on what he'd heard, she often did.

In fact, Delilah was a common topic in the men's locker room. He wasn't the only one she'd flirted with. Several had openly wondered why Mack — who reputedly had zero tolerance for that kind of thing — didn't fire her outright. That was when one of the guys revealed that Delilah was actually Mack's stepsister, and the only reason she kept Delilah around was as a personal favor to her father.

Nick felt a flash of irritation on Mack's behalf. If that were true (and he had no reason to believe it wasn't), that was a hell of a situation to put someone in, family or not.

"The Covendale PD is so lucky to have you," Delilah said. "I read about what you did last year. You're a bona fide hero!"

Nick grimaced, able to guess what she was

referring to. That had been a shit show all around. A double-crossing informant had fed them some bad info, turning an eight-month sting operation into a deadly trap meant to obliterate their whole vice team. Thankfully, Nick had some (far more reliable) sources of his own who tipped him off, and he managed to get there just as they were about to storm the multi-million dollar, underground pharmaceutical lab. The guy in charge, an arrogant, self-important asshole named Carter, had refused to listen and just seconds after the first men entered the facility, the place blew. Nick managed to pull a couple guys to safety, but he was by no means the only one. The papers, however, credited him with saving not only the lives of those who he'd carried out, but also the dozens of others who *would* have been inside had he not delayed the operation by arguing with Carter.

Two good men died in that explosion, several more had been injured, and Carter had been relieved of his command. There was nothing heroic about it.

"I read about what happened around here, too," she added, lowering her voice, her predatory grin turning to one offering false comfort. "You must have been devastated. It must be really hard on you, coming back here. I'm a good listener, if you ever need to … talk."

Nick ground his molars, unwilling to hear any more of what Delilah had to say. "I'm looking for Mack. Is she around?"

Delilah's eyes flashed. Just that quickly, her sympathetic smile morphed into a well-practiced pout. "I haven't seen her."

She was lying, Nick was certain of it. Another thing he was certain of? Delilah didn't like being blown off.

He didn't bother thanking her, resolving to find Mack on his own.

He swung by the teen center first, but Mack wasn't there. He declined an offer of a pick-up game and asked the kids if they'd seen Mack. That's how he discovered she was sparring down in one of the MMA rooms.

"Awesome, Fucker. Thanks," Mack said, her voice laced with genuine affection as she tugged off her gloves. The towering blond Viking shot her a brilliant smile and offered her a casual salute. "Anytime, Mack."

Nick, who had caught the last few minutes of the session, blinked in disbelief.

"You call him *Fucker*?" he asked, following Mack away from the mats. The woman barely came up to the Thor lookalike's chest, yet she'd managed to hold her own, using her small size and impressive knowledge of leverage to her advantage.

"He's Norwegian," she shrugged, as if that explained it all.

"So? You got something against Norwegians?"

She rolled her eyes. Again, he found that one small action arousing, just as he did the sheen of perspiration shimmering over her skin and the wisps of hair that clung to the base of her neck, showcasing that heart-shaped mark beneath her jaunty ponytail. In fact, he found nearly everything about Mack arousing. But his appreciation went deeper than that. He wanted to learn more about the intriguing woman inside the enticing package.

"His name is Lars Volker," she told him. "*Volker*, with a "V", but when he says it in his Scandinavian accent—the way it was meant to be said—it sounds more like 'fucker' in English."

Well, he supposed that made sense. "He doesn't mind?"

She tilted her head back and drank deeply from her water bottle. Nick had to force his eyes away from the way her throat, shiny and slick with moisture, moved up and down with the action. Not his best idea, since his gaze naturally dropped to her well-endowed chest, her sweaty '*Seize* the Day' tank plastered against all that perfectly smooth, lickable skin. The woman wasn't even trying and she was making him hard. On the plus side, she didn't seem to be openly avoiding him as he had suspected earlier that morning.

"No. I think he likes it. Makes him feel like a badass." When Mack grinned, her whole face lit up, making him feel like smiling, too. "Besides, there are worse nicknames than that."

"Yeah? Like what?" He liked this playful banter. He liked talking to her, anticipating what she would say next. "Well, this one guy was named Joel Lipschitz, and they called him—"

He held up a hand to stop her. "I'm sorry I

asked."

She grinned again, her eyes twinkling with a little bit of mischief and a whole lot of naughty. "And then there was this Asian guy. One hell of a demolitions expert, best I've ever seen. We called him Nads."

"Jesus, do I even want to know?"

"Probably not. His actual name was Hung Lo."

It took a moment for him to make the connection, but when he did, he nearly doubled over in laughter. God, he liked this woman! Just five minutes with her and he felt lighter, more alive than he had in weeks.

"What about you?" he teased when he could speak again. "Did you have a nickname, too?"

The laughter faded from her eyes and she turned her attention to something else. "Just Mack."

"Liar." He pointed at himself. "Detective, remember? I'm trained to tell when someone is trying to hand me a load of bullshit." He playfully bumped her shoulder.

He tried to ignore the shock of heat that radiated out from that slight, completely innocent contact. Judging by the way her eyes had widened, she had felt it, too. She didn't look happy about it, though.

"What are the chances of you dropping this?"

"Slim and none," he replied. "Come on, you can tell me."

"Nothing to tell."

"I have my ways. Spill, woman."

She rolled her eyes again and huffed. "Mack.

Short for MacKenzie. My last name. See? No big deal."

He blinked. "Wait. MacKenzie is your *last* name? I thought it was your first name."

"Nope." She turned and started walking toward the water cooler to refill her eco-bottle.

"So," he pushed, following along behind her. "What is your first name?"

Chapter Sixteen

~ *Mack* ~

Damn it! What was it about Nick Benning that made her go weak in the knees like some swooning girly-girl? Was it his boy-next-door smile? His have-sex-with-me-and-I'll-make-it-the-best-you-ever-had eyes? Or simply the way her body lit up whenever he was within striking distance?

Resisting him took effort. The man could coax the habit off a nun when he turned on the charm. He probably didn't even realize he was doing it. For some guys, oozing sex appeal was as autonomic as breathing, and Nick Benning had it in spades.

Corralling her wandering hormones, Mack looked at him with mock seriousness and lowered her voice. "I'd tell you, but then I'd have to kill you."

He laughed, a deep rich sound that rippled

through her lower core. "Come on. It's not a state secret, is it?"

She bit her lip. A state secret, no, but not something she normally shared. Delilah knew, of course. And Jay. Beyond that, there really wasn't anyone close enough to tell or who had cared enough to ask. Not even her father called her by her given name. Well, not unless the crafty old codger was laying a major guilt trip and attempting to cash in every father-daughter chip he had.

"Tell me." He leaned forward, close enough that she could smell the cool mintiness of his breath and see the light dusting of shadow along his jawline.

"Why?"

"I'm curious."

"I imagine that's a good trait in your line of work."

"I feel like I'm at a disadvantage here. You know *my* first name. I'm even willing to provide my home address and credit card information."

Her lips quirked. If he became a permanent member (and there was no reason to think he wouldn't), he would provide all of that information and more on his application. But that was all business. She would never use that for personal reasons. When she still said nothing, he added, "I brought you coffee."

Ah, yes, the coffee. The quirk became a smile. That had been a pleasant surprise, coming back to the front desk to find a dark chocolate mocha with a shot of espresso waiting for her. It was exactly what she'd needed after her restless night and her morning clash with Princess Dee.

The grilling that cup of coffee had elicited, however, wasn't nearly as enjoyable. Chrissy was still in the grips of the magical honeymoon phase and saw romance in even the most innocuous of gestures. Mack had tried to tell her that it wasn't like that, but then she'd had to explain about their wager, which Chrissy insisted was like a munitions-centric form of foreplay.

"Yes, you did," she agreed. "Thanks for that, by the way."

"You're welcome. I'm sorry I didn't make it to O'Malley's in time."

"No apology necessary."

"So you said." His momentary frown suggested he did not agree. "Now stop trying to change the subject. Tell me your first name."

"No."

"Please?" he said softly, leaning even closer. Mack held her breath, afraid to take in any more of his scent. Nick's fragrant men's soap and deodorant was like crack to her jonesing libido, weakening her defenses. "I could look it up, of course, but I'd rather hear it from you."

Her resolve was wavering. Maybe she could tell him. He was trying to be friendly, and friends did that kind of thing, right? It could even be like an inside joke between them, something the two of them shared but no one else knew. She licked her lips and opened her mouth to speak.

"Nick! There you are!" Dee's sultry voice cut

through Mack's Nick-induced brain fog just seconds before the woman herself sashayed up and grasped his arm in an obvious claim. "You walked away before I had a chance to give you my number."

Nick's reaction was instant. He straightened, all traces of playfulness vanishing as he turned around to greet Dee. The interruption was a much-needed reality check, cutting through whatever ridiculous, pheromone-induced fog had temporarily hijacked her common sense.

Dee looked stunning, as usual, with her blonde extensions artfully braided and just enough bronzer to give her a healthy, radiant glow. Mack lowered her gaze self-consciously, taking in her plain wicking tank and unflattering shorts and her limbs slick with real sweat instead of the spritzed on, glittery kind.

Mack couldn't compete with Dee, nor did she want to. If a man was incapable of looking beneath the surface, then he wasn't worth her time.

"Nice, Mack," Delilah said, wrinkling her nose at her. "Most people change into a bathing suit before they go swimming."

Clearly, Delilah was still upset over Mack's refusal to do her bidding. Rather than tell Dee what she really thought — they had an audience, after all — Mack opted for self-effacing humor. "Come on, Dee. No one wants to see that."

Dee's smile was like that of a shark's as her eyes raked down Mack's form — cold and predatory. Mack saw the virtual blade unsheathing and braced herself for the blow that came a second later. "Good point. Don't you have some guys to beat up or something?"

Nick stiffened, no doubt a result of the awkward, rising tension, and Mack decided to make it easier on everyone. "As a matter of fact, I do." Mack turned back to Nick, forcing a smile. "Nice talking to you, Detective. Enjoy the rest of your evening."

Mack made a quick getaway before she said or did something she would regret, like kick Dee's smug, arrogant ass across the mats.

She grabbed her stuff and headed home, but first she stopped at the front desk and inactivated Dee's card. The moment Delilah walked out those doors, her brief employment at *Seize* was officially terminated.

Jay watched as she moved the small watering can over the layered planters that took up a good third of the spacious kitchen. Fashioned like a spiral staircase, a bounty of fresh herbs and spices rose from the tiled terra cotta floor all the way up to the open dark wood beams. Mack often found comfort in tending to her multitude of gardens inside and out, and Jay knew this.

"So," he said, grabbing a handful of dried apple slices from the dehydrator as he followed her. "I saw you talking to the new guy again today."

"Yeah? So?" she shrugged before catching the gleam in his eye. "He works out at *Seize*. We're bound to cross paths occasionally."

"Uh-huh."

"Wipe that smirk off your face. It's not like he's seeking me out, Jay."

"Of course not."

She exhaled. "Look, tonight I bumped into him after sparring with Volker. Before that, I saw him in the weight room a couple times. No big deal."

He narrowed his eyes. "What were you doing in the weight room?"

"Duh. Lifting weights."

Jay looked at her sternly. "We talked about this, Mack."

"No, *you* talked about this. I pretended to listen and then completely disregarded your appreciated but totally misguided advice. Lots of women lift weights. It builds lean muscle and helps prevent osteoporosis later in life."

"They lift little pink weights in LuLaRoe to bad techno pop, not deadlift in camo to heavy metal."

Mack smirked; he knew her so well.

"Seriously, Mack. You're completely repressing your feminine side. Do some sexy pole dancing in between the power squats once in a while, you know?"

She shook her head. She didn't mind doing that kind of stuff in private classes, but not in public. "No. That's not me."

"Why not? You have a V-card, don't you? You didn't exchange it for a P while you were over in Europe?"

Mack straightened from her crouch and threw a weed at his head. "Fucktard. Can you imagine this —" she waved her hands up and down her body "—

shaking it with a bunch of spandex-clad Pluto booties?"

"Pluto booties?"

"Yeah. Girls with butts so small they're practically nonexistent." The ones that made Mack feel like a linebacker just because she had some meat on her bones.

Jay gaped at her. "Are you seriously saying you have a fat ass?"

"No. But this baby's got back. *You* take twenty-mile mountain hikes carrying fifty pounds of gear and see what kind of glutes you get."

"Turn around," he commanded, spinning an apple slice in the air. She did. Jay brought his fingers to his chin and looked at her critically.

"Yeah, I see what you mean. Nice ass, Mack."

"I know, right?"

"No, baby girl, the problem is, you *don't* know. You have no idea how guys look at you. If you gave them even one iota of encouragement they'd be swarming out of the woodwork, but you keep them at a distance. I am the only one you allow close enough to see past that intense 'don't mess with me' attitude and into your Texas-size heart. It's frustrating."

That was, quite possibly, one of the nicest things anyone had ever said to her. Mack blinked rapidly several times, but kept her expression neutral. "Thanks, Jay. I appreciate the effort. But you know as well as I do that your opinion as my housemate and BFF isn't realistic. Beyond trying to cheer me up, it's completely biased."

"Just promise me you'll think about letting your inner diva out once in a while. You already do private classes. Do a public class, Mack. Just one. Look at it this way: at the very least, it's great cardio and you might actually have fun."

She snorted at that. "Public humiliation is not fun." Ask her to navigate an obstacle course? Run ten miles? Drop and pound out fifty pushups? Yeah, she was all over that. Attempt a body roll in front of a wall full of mirrors and twenty snickering females? Not so much.

"Hot guys would line up in the hallway and watch," Jay told her.

"That's just one more excellent reason not to."

"What? You're not interested in guys now?"

Mack winced, remembering her earlier conversation with Dee. She looked around Jay, half-expecting to see Dee nodding her head and gleefully chanting, "I knew it!" Then another image muscled in, the one of Dee linking her arm through Nick's with another triumphant smile. Mack hadn't stuck around to see what happened. At that very moment, Princess Dee might even be getting in *her* body rolls beneath the hot detective. The modicum of Zen Mack had achieved by tending to her herbs vanished instantly.

"In the first place, that's a form of harassment."

"Appreciation is not harassment."

"And in the second place, no. Just… no. I love you, Jay, I do, but stop trying to make me into something I'm not, okay?"

His face grew serious. "You know better than

that, Mack."

Yeah, she did, but she was tired and cranky and done with the conversation. "Just... give it a rest, okay?"

"All right, baby girl. But I'm always here for you."

"I know. Thanks."

Chapter Seventeen

~ Nick ~

Nick watched Mack walk away, resisting the urge to follow.

Delilah licked her lips and flexed her nails against into his forearm like claws, despite the fact that he'd removed them only a minute earlier.

"Let me be very clear about this, Delilah, so there is no misunderstanding," he said, firmly removing her hand. "I am not interested."

She blinked as if confused. 'No' was probably not a word she heard often. Her eyes moved toward the door Mack had just exited.

"But you're interested in *Mack*?" she asked in stunned disbelief.

Hell yes, he was, but Nick wasn't about to share that — or anything else — with Delilah. "I'm interested in finishing my workout. Now, if you'll excuse me."

Turning away from Delilah and her scowl,

Nick's first inclination was to go after Mack. To seek her out and do whatever it took to put that playful sparkle back into her eyes.

He didn't, though. Not because he didn't want to, but because he didn't think Mack would want him to. They hadn't reached that stage yet.

Instead, he set a course for the cardio deck and relieved some of his simmering angst in the form of a full-out run. His heart wasn't in it, though, and after just a few miles, he hit the showers. His evening plans now included looking more into the Necromancers and maybe texting Mack. Nothing heavy, just something to open up the lines of communication again and get some dialogue going. Maybe something simple, like asking how her class went or following through on his do-over request.

On his way out, he saw Delilah again, only this time, she didn't spare him more than a passing glance. She was giving most of her attention to Kent Emerson, who didn't seem to mind her attention at all. That was just fine with Nick. In fact, the two seemed well-suited for each other.

"Detective, wait up."

Nick slowed his pace across the lot as Mack's housemate, Jay, jogged up to him. "Did you make use of those digits?"

"I did," Nick confirmed. "Thanks for that."

"No problem. Chrissy told me about the coffee this morning. Very smooth."

Nick laughed. "Thanks. Hey, you wouldn't happen to know Mack's first name, would you?"

Jay eyes twinkled with mischief. "Maybe."

"Care to share?"

"I don't know if I should. What exactly are your intentions, young man?"

Nick shrugged. "Just looking to make a friend, that's all."

"That's all?" Jay asked skeptically.

"No," he admitted. "But that'll do, for now."

Jay said nothing for several moments, then nodded. "Fair enough. Mack's first name is Heather."

Heather MacKenzie. Nick rolled the name around in his mind. It fit Mack to a "T". Strong and beautiful, just like her. His mother was particularly fond of the plant and used to have several bushes around their front porch. In the winter, she kept the fragrant dried sprigs around the house for good luck. The scent of heather still filled him with feelings of comfort and warmth. Was that some kind of cosmic sign, he wondered?

"Thanks, Jay."

"Knowledge is power, Detective. Use it wisely."

Jay's subtle warning echoed in his head as he cruised through town, puzzling out the best way to engage Mack when he caught a glimpse of what looked like his classic Shelby disappearing around the corner, drawing his instant and complete attention.

Could that be his baby? Was Liz finally back in town?

Nick turned the corner and stepped on the gas, closing the distance between them. He might have been mistaken, but it was doubtful. He'd spent too many hours lovingly restoring every inch of that car; he knew each curve and dip as well as he knew his own body.

He caught up to it right before it left the limits of the town proper. It *was* his baby, he was sure of it. But it definitely wasn't Liz driving it.

Nick flipped the switch on his dash, turning his Charger into an identifiable police vehicle. Alternately flashing headlights and blue flashers hidden discreetly behind the front grill came to life. The Shelby's blinkers went on in acknowledgement, and the driver pulled off to the side of the road when the shoulder was wide enough to safely do so.

Nick parked behind the car, verifying the license number. Then he exited the vehicle and walked up to where the driver had rolled down the window. It was a kid! Male Caucasian, clean-cut. Early twenties. Dark hair, blue eyes that held confusion.

"Driver's license and registration, please," Nick demanded, producing his badge. "And keep your hands where I can see them."

The kid's eyes widened. "My wallet's in my back pocket. The registration is in the glove compartment. I need to reach for both."

Smart kid. Nick nodded in acknowledgement. "Slowly, please."

"Can I ask what this is about, Officer?"

Nick didn't answer him right away. He waited until he had the kid's license in hand. "Are you aware of the penalty for stealing a car —" Nick looked at the license "— Brandon?"

"You think I *stole* this car?"

The kid handed over the registration. Nick's eyes narrowed. The registration had the kid's name on it. So did the insurance. Both were up to date and looked legit.

"Where did you get this vehicle?"

"It was a graduation present."

"From?"

"Liz. I mean Elizabeth. Elizabeth Benning. I mean, Elizabeth Grayson."

"Elizabeth *Grayson*?"

"Yeah, my father's wife."

Liz was *married*?

Nick tried to keep the shock from his face. "She will verify this?"

"Yeah, of course. We can call her right now if you want, but I'm not sure she'll answer. They're on their honeymoon, kind of an around the world thing. I think they're in Tokyo this week."

Well, that explained why Liz hadn't been answering her phone or her door. Nick didn't know what surprised him more: the fact that Liz gave his car away or that she was married and on her honeymoon.

"Officer? Are you okay?"

"Detective," Nick answered automatically.

"Detective Nick Benning."

"Benning? Are you related to Liz? Holy sh—. You're her brother, aren't you?"

Nick nodded.

"You didn't know."

"No." But he *should* have. A brother should definitely know when his only sister gets *married*. "You wouldn't happen to know when Liz is getting back, would you?"

"Not until the end of the summer."

It was awkward, standing there beside his prized Shelby with someone else behind the wheel. Curious motorists were slowing down, rubbernecking to see what was going on. No doubt a few were capturing the moment on their smart phones, too. Even shaken as he was, he knew the side of the road was no place for this conversation.

"Thanks, Brandon. Sorry about the misunderstanding."

"No problem. This must be pretty weird for you, huh?"

Weird. Yeah. More like a sucker punch to the gut.

Nick wished Brandon a good night, then got into his car and drove back to his place, feeling stunned by the unexpected turn of events. He tried to wrap his mind around it, but wasn't having much luck.

Liz was *married*.

And she'd *given his car away*. His car. His *baby*.

Had Liz even tried to reach him? Or had she

written him out of her life, given up on him completely?

He couldn't blame her if she had. The tragedy all those years ago must have been hard on them, too. He'd left, but his family had had to deal with the daily reminders. Liz had once told him that yeah, he'd lost Annie, but she and their parents had lost *him* because of what happened, and that hurt, too.

He hadn't fully understood what she'd been saying then. They hadn't lost him. He was still alive, even if he wasn't part of their day-to-day lives. Liz understood that he needed time and space, at least at first. She kept those early communications short and sweet. Wishing him a happy birthday. Reminding him of their parents' anniversary. Letting him know they'd sold the house and were retiring to Florida.

He should have responded beyond the obligatory annual birthday and anniversary wishes.

At first, it had been too painful, each card, letter, and text reminding him of what he'd lost. Then he'd thrown himself into his job, working sixteen-hour days and thinking of little else. After a while, Liz stopped calling and writing altogether.

It begged the question, what else didn't he know?

The kid — Brandon — had given him Liz's cell number to substantiate his story, but there was no doubt in Nick's mind that the kid was telling the truth.

The microwave dinged, letting him know that his dinner was ready. As he sat at the counter with his reheated takeout, Nick thumbed his phone and sighed. He wasn't going to call Liz. Not when she was on her *honeymoon*. Nick had waited more than ten years to have this conversation; he could wait another month and a half. Besides, he wasn't planning on going anywhere.

Instead, another face came to mind. His thumb tapped out a text message. *"You there?"*

Chapter Eighteen

~ *Mack* ~

Mack let the hot water soothe her aching muscles. She'd overdone it, ramping up the weights more than she should have. But damn it, she'd needed to get rid of some of that extra energy somehow. She'd been doing so good – Volker had really challenged her, pushing her to her limits – and then *he* had to show up.

Damn Nick and his flippin' perfect white teeth, male model physique, and potent pheromones! She was not some silly little girl! She was a grown woman with a productive and satisfying life. The last thing she needed was a man screwing things up.

It was stupid – really, really stupid – to feel this way about someone she barely knew. So what if his eyes made her insides feel as though they were melting when they focused on her? So what if her heart picked up speed and her entire body felt hyper-aware whenever he was in the same room?

So what if the mere scent of him made some parts of her rhythmically clench without conscious thought?

Even knowing how stupid it was, she was powerless against it. No one else had ever affected her this way. She had no frame of reference for how to deal with it.

It was more than insta-lust inspired by his good looks. She was surrounded by buff, handsome men all the time – first in the service, then at the gym. While she had — very discreetly — admired several of them, it had never felt like *this*. Like she wanted to spend hours just talking to him, learning about him, taking him up into the mountains. Just plain taking him.

Fantasizing about getting hot and sweaty between the sheets was one thing, but wanting to share her mountain with him? That had her shaken.

But why shouldn't she think about those things, another part of her wondered? Nick Benning wasn't just another handsome-faced and buff-bodied hero type. He was also funny and playful, and when he hit her with those amazing eyes she felt as if he could see past all the surface stuff and really *see* her.

No one had ever done that before.

Mack ignored the hopeful, romantic voices in her head, after telling them to shut the hell up. This wasn't a Disney movie. Nick Benning was *not* Prince Charming, and she was no goddamn princess.

Oh, at one time, she'd dreamed of all the same

things little girls dreamed of – falling in love, getting married, having kids, living happily ever after. She'd found out soon enough that fairy tales weren't nearly as fun when you had to deal with a real-life stepmother and stepsister. Especially when the stepsister was the charming, beautiful one and she was the one staying home on Saturday nights.

That naïve little girl was long gone. In her place was a much stronger, much smarter woman who led a full and productive life. She had her own successful business doing what she loved. A beautiful house and the best housemate anyone could wish for. She was active in the community.

She had no reason to sit around feeling sorry for herself because of something someone else did or said. It was time to get her head on straight, whip her AWOL senses back into shape, and suck it up like the proud, capable Marine she was.

Being in the service had transformed her. She liked the discipline. Liked the grueling twelve-week recruit training that gave her a sense of accomplishment, just for having survived it. Was elated when she passed the ASVAB tests with the highest scores in her class. She basked in the unconditional support of her team. The Marines had turned her from a nobody into somebody.

And that somebody was a badass who did *not* sit home pining over some guy.

No longer was she the shy, quiet, chubby girl that elicited the snickers and taunts of her peers or was the recipient of more than a few cruel practical jokes. She was *Mack* now; not Chubby, Fatty,

Loser, or Thunderbutt.

She would never be thin, never be tall, never be a great beauty, but that was okay. She liked looking at herself in the mirror, seeing the radiant glow of good health, her natural curves highlighted with toned muscle underneath. Screw what everyone else thought.

Right?

She'd come so far. The physical changes had been epic. No one who knew her before she enlisted would ever recognize her now, and she took a lot of pride in that. It had taken years to get to this point. Years of hard work, sweat, sometimes tears, and a boatload of self-denial.

And yet - despite all that she had accomplished – it only took a few casually tossed barbs from Dee to rattle her. Maybe a little piece of the girl she'd once been still lived inside her after all. The one who knew that no matter how many friends she had, no matter how many men would want her at their six, they would never look at her the way they looked at Dee.

At the end of the day, insecurity was coded right into the strands of her DNA.

She'd learned to hide it well over the years, bury it beneath layers and layers of sass and attitude. No one ever knew or even suspected that it still hurt, not when she'd grown such a thick skin. Skin that obviously wasn't always thick enough.

When the water grew cool, Mack released the stopper and began to towel off. That was when she saw the light on her phone blinking, indicating a message. That was also about the time when her heart started doing this weird pitter-patter thing.

It was probably just Jay, telling her he was going to be home late and not to worry. Or maybe someone from *Seize*, calling with a question or an issue. There was no reason to think it was *him*, yet she knew it was.

She wrapped the towel around her body self-consciously. Given her lack of digital skills, she was likely to tap the video button accidentally and flash her contact list with a visual of hard nipples and pruney skin.

Mack inhaled sharply when she woke up the screen and saw it.

Nick: *You there?*

It *was* from him. What could he possibly want? When she'd left him at the gym, it had been with Dee wrapped around his arm. Her traitorous fingers were tapping out a reply before her mind could convince them it was a bad idea.

Mack: *Yeah, what's up?*

Mack tossed the phone on her bed (just to prove to herself she could) and pulled on some comfortable sleepwear. She'd barely finished when the light was blinking again.

Nick: *Meet for coffee? My treat.*

She smiled. He was persistent. And, if he was asking her for coffee, that meant he *wasn't with Dee*. Was it possible that the good detective was one of the few men capable of seeing past the double-D's and blatant come-ons? The thought shouldn't have made her as happy as it did.

Mack: *What is it with you and coffee?*

The reply came back immediately.

Nick: *I'm a cop. Do the math.*

She laughed.

Mack: *If I meet you for coffee, will that ease your guilty conscience?*

Nick: *Maybe…*

They made plans to meet at Ground Zero in thirty minutes. Feeling oddly rejuvenated, Mack pulled on some jeans and a t-shirt. She gave her hair a quick brushing, telling herself not to make a big deal out of it. It was just a friendly cup of coffee, nothing more.

Unlike last time, Nick was already there when she arrived, waiting for her in the parking lot. His eyes lit on her the moment she pulled in, and he was there to open the door for her as soon as she'd turned the car off.

Thus far, she'd seen him in a suit and in workout gear, and he'd looked good in both. But in jeans and a white button down with the sleeves rolled back and some serious shadow gracing his strong jawline, he looked even better. When a light breeze teased locks of dark golden hair onto his forehead, she fought the urge to brush them back.

"Thanks for meeting me," he said.

"You're a persistent man."

"I can be," he agreed.

"And stubborn, too. I told you, you don't need to do this."

He exhaled. "Ever think that maybe I just want to?"

"Why?"

He opened the door to the coffee shop and stood back, allowing her to go in first. "You're not going to make this easy, are you?"

The words "make what easy?" almost crossed her lips before she stopped them and turned her attention to the menu board. He ordered a large black coffee and a jelly doughnut; she got an herbal tea.

At that hour, the place was only about half full and they were able to find an empty table easily enough. Mack was pleased when he selected a table in the corner where they could both sit with their backs to the wall near the back. She liked to see everyone coming and going and as a cop, he probably did, too.

"So," she asked once they were settled. "How do you like Covendale? Is it everything you'd hoped for and more?"

Chapter Nineteen

~ *Nick* ~

He liked that playful twinkle in her eye and smiled, silently appreciating the fact that *she* was the 'and more' and didn't even realize it. "Definitely. It hasn't changed much."

"You've been here before?"

He nodded. "I grew up here."

"Is that why you came back? To be around your family?"

"That's part of it," he answered. "My sister still lives in town, but she's currently on her honeymoon." The knowledge still rankled. "My parents retired to Florida years ago."

He liked that she was asking questions. He sat back and let her take the lead, pleased that she seemed genuinely interested in his answers. Her attention was solely on him, not roaming around the café.

"What about friends? Is it weird, reconnecting

with people you haven't seen for a while? Like a class reunion that never ends?"

He laughed. Fortunately or unfortunately, he hadn't met up with many old acquaintances since he'd returned. After Annie died, he'd withdrawn from everyone and everything, and most of those connections had been severed before he'd even left.

"I've lost touch with most of the people I knew then. Right now, in fact, you are on a very short list of people I want to hang out with."

"Me?" Her widened eyes and genuine surprise were adorable.

"Yes, you."

She raised her mug and sipped her tea. He remained silent while she wrapped her mind around that. Then she cleared her throat and quietly said, "Same."

"Yeah?"

"Yeah." She shrugged as if it was no big deal but it was to him. It definitely felt like a much-needed check in his win column.

He barely had a chance to celebrate that minor victory when she followed up with, "So why'd you leave? Small town life not exciting enough for you?"

Unlike her sister, Mack hadn't gone digging. She didn't know about his tormented past. If only he could have kept it that way for a little while longer. He tried to keep his smile when he replied, "Just the opposite."

He must not have done a very good job of it, because her teasing smile faded and she cast her eyes back to her tea. "I'm sorry, I shouldn't have asked. It's none of my business."

Nick didn't like talking about what happened, but if he was serious about wanting to pursue something with her (and he was), he wanted her to know.

"No, it's okay. A simple Google search will tell you everything you want to know."

She wrinkled up her nose and shook her head. "Cyberstalking isn't my style. Besides, it's not like you can believe everything you read on the internet."

"You're a wise and special woman, Heather MacKenzie."

Her eyes opened wide at the deliberate use of her first name. Then she smiled. "Touché, Detective. I don't suppose you're going to tell me who ratted me out?"

"A good detective never reveals his sources." He winked. "As far as why I left..."

Mack put her hand over his and looked him in the eye. "You don't owe me any explanations, Nick."

Two things registered in that moment. One, she was touching him, and that simple contact infused him with a warmth and comfort he hadn't felt in a very long time. And two, she had called him by his first name.

He looked down at her hand, trapping it when she tried to pull away. "I know. I want to tell you. Covendale is a small town, so it's bound to come up eventually. I'd rather you hear it from me."

She nodded. "Okay."

"About ten years ago, my fiancée was killed in a car accident. She died believing that I was unfaithful."

"That's awful!"

"It is," he agreed. "I was at a holiday party. She worked second shift at the hospital and was supposed to come later after she got off work. But someone slipped something into my drink and set it up so that when Annie showed up, it looked as if I had cheated on her with someone else."

Mack's brows drew together. "A jealous ex?" she guessed.

"Jealous, yes. Ex, no. I was never interested in Eve Sanderson. Unfortunately, the feeling wasn't mutual and she didn't like taking no for an answer."

Mack's lips thinned. "Sounds like an entitled bitch."

"In a nutshell."

"Wait… Eve Sanderson. She was just in the news not too long ago. She roofied a local man and tried to blow up his girlfriend." Her eyes widened as she connected the dots. "Oh my God. Nick, I'm so sorry."

"Thank you. It happened a long time ago."

"Grief doesn't punch a time card."

"Spoken like someone who truly understands."

She shrugged. This time when she tried to pull her hand away, he let her. "I lost my mother a long time ago, too, but it still hurts. I still miss her. So yeah, I get it."

The conversation had taken a dark turn. Nick

didn't like the sadness in her eyes, and he didn't want to talk about Annie anymore. Maybe someday he'd feel comfortable revealing more, but the subject was too heavy for their first coffee date.

"What about you? What brought you to this tiny hidden valley in the middle of nowhere?"

Her expression cleared slightly. "I like the natural beauty, I guess. Mountains, valleys, rivers, lakes. The unpredictability of four distinct seasons."

"Outdoorsy type, huh?"

"Definitely. Give me a mountain trail over a paved road any day."

"A woman after my own heart. I knew I sensed a kindred spirit."

She smiled, her features softening into that comfortable, relaxed look she'd had earlier before it grew wistful.

"I like the small town vibe, too. It reminds me of where I lived as a child, before my dad moved us to the west coast."

"And what about *Seize*? Life-long dream?"

"Not exactly. I didn't know what I wanted to do with my life. I joined the Marines after high school, found my focus, and the rest, as they say, is history. Did you always want to be a detective?"

"A Marine, huh? That's impressive." She beamed. "To answer your question, no," he told her with a serious face. "When I was seven I wanted to be a famous race car driver. Or Batman."

She laughed and the mood lifted again. Talking with Mack was so easy, as if they had known each other for years instead of hours. They covered a variety of topics including music, movies, and food choices. Unsurprisingly, they liked many of the same things.

Before he knew it, it was midnight. As much as he didn't want the night to end, they both had early mornings ahead of them.

"Thanks for having coffee with me tonight, Mack."

"Thanks for asking."

"Maybe we can do it again sometime."

He held his breath as her eyes lifted and met his. In that moment, the rest of the world faded away. Nick felt a new level of connection fire to life between them, something deeper and stronger than the simple pull of attraction he'd felt before.

"I'd like that," she answered softly.

The urge to kiss her was strong. To pull her close and put his lips to hers. To feel her body pressed against his, knowing she would fit perfectly.

Then she broke eye contact and the moment was over.

Nick mentally kicked himself for not taking advantage of the moment, but perhaps it was better that he hadn't. Anticipation was supposed to be a good thing, right? Next time, however, he wouldn't hesitate.

They said goodnight. He watched her drive away, feeling better than he had a couple of hours earlier. Not much had changed. He was still going home to an empty house. He still had to deal with the fact that the Necromancers were selling drugs to kids. His precious Shelby belonged to someone else and his sister had gone and gotten married without him knowing. But inside, he felt ... lighter.

And it was all because of Mack.

She was an excellent listener. Beautiful, intelligent, well-spoken, strong. Passionate about what she loved – and didn't. And he'd only scratched the surface. He couldn't wait to dig deeper, discover more. Now that he'd taken that first step, he was anxious to keep going.

The same instincts that made him a good detective suggested that Mack was interested, too, but he wasn't sure he could trust that. He'd been out of the game for a long time. It was also possible that his own wishful thinking was influencing his perception. The one thing he did know for certain was that he wanted to see where this thing with Mack would lead.

He thought about texting her when he got back to his place. Nothing quick, just something quick to confirm that he'd enjoyed the evening and wanted to see her again. Then he was going to do a thorough background check on Miles Grayson, his new *brother-in-law*.

He'd no sooner walked in the door, however, than his cell phone went off.

"Nick? Sam Brown. I need you to get over to the hospital. It's Jesse."

Nick turned around and got right back into his car, his stomach clenching into a knot. "On my way. Is he okay?"

"I'll fill you in when you get here."

Nick made it to the hospital in record time. He found Sam Brown waiting for him. "What happened?"

Sam's face was grim. "Apparently, Jesse Sr. isn't willing to let go so easily. He sent some of his club brethren over to the house to remind his wife of that. Jesse Jr. tried to show them the door, got a few broken bones and some nice bruises for his troubles. Luckily, the mother called 9-1-1 the moment she saw them at the door and help arrived before they could do any worse. She's with Jesse now."

"Jesus. The attackers?"

"Got two of them in custody, but I don't know how long they're going to stay there. The club's got some slick lawyer already pushing to get them out. More restraining orders are being drafted as we speak, but…"

Chief Brown didn't have to finish that statement. They already knew what the Necromancers thought of restraining orders. From his research, Nick knew the club had their own set of laws, and those were the only ones that mattered. Among them: women and children claimed by patched members belonged to those members to do with as they pleased, period. It was misogyny at its worst.

"We've got to get them somewhere safe until we take care of this. Somewhere off the grid where the Necromancers won't be able to get to them."

"Agreed." Sam rubbed at his jaw, now covered in thick, reddish-brown stubble. "I've got a hunting cabin up in Potter County."

"That'll do. I can take them up as soon as the doc releases Jesse."

"I was hoping you'd say that. I'll call Gail, have her gather up supplies to take with you."

Chapter Twenty

~ *Mack* ~

Mack stared at the screen and exhaled. She wasn't proud of what she'd done. Was this what her errant female hormones had reduced her to?

She blamed Nick. Ever since their coffee date she'd been thinking crazy things. Like maybe she'd actually found a guy (besides Jay) who enjoyed her company. Someone who she liked, as well. Someone with whom a friendship might blossom into something more.

She'd thought that guy might just be Nick Benning.

That was days ago. Now, she wasn't quite as hopeful as she'd been. She'd thought their 'date' had gone well, but Nick hadn't called since. He hadn't texted. They hadn't crossed paths at *Seize*. Mack had to be realistic and consider the possibility that Nick was simply a nice, friendly guy who didn't share the same powerful attraction to her as she had to him.

It wouldn't be the first time. Some women were just meant to stay in the friend zone, what Mack liked to refer to as the 'always a bridesmaid' phenomenon. Except in Mack's case, she didn't have a lot of female friends so she had never been (and probably never would be) a bridesmaid, either.

That realization, along with a sprinkling of self-pity and a few glasses of wine, had prompted her to take action.

"I'm home!" Mack startled at the sound of Jay announcing his arrival, Thank God it was him and not Dee. If Dee saw her on a singles match site she'd never hear the end of it.

Then again, Dee hadn't been around much. She'd been keeping herself scarce ever since Mack officially fired her. That conversation hadn't been as satisfying as she'd imagined, because Dee told her that she'd already received a call back from Tish and was planning on quitting anyway. That was okay with Mack. She no longer had to worry about Dee harassing clients or screwing things up and making everyone else's job harder.

Another bonus: since Mack spent most of her time at *Seize*, her interactions with Dee were limited and more easily managed. Dee was no longer expected to rise at the 'ass crack of dawn' (as she'd put it), so she slept in and stayed out late, which further minimized face time. The less time, the better, in Mack's opinion.

"Why aren't you answering your phone?"

Mack looked at the dark, silent phone next to her. She'd been keeping it nearby, 'just in case' Nick happened to text. "It didn't ring."

Jay came over and took a look. "That's because it's out of charge again."

"Can't be. I haven't even used it."

He scowled, tapping and swiping the screen. "Jesus, Mack. You've got like fifty-two open windows and six apps running. Don't you ever close them down?"

"I thought I did. I just press the home key, right?"

He shook his head. "No, genius. You've got to actually *close* the windows. You know, 'x' marks the spot? That's what is running down your battery."

Huh.

"And what the hell, Mack? Why are you using my wireless charger as a coaster?"

She looked over at the small black disk, the one her empty wine glass was now sitting on. It sure *looked* like a coaster. Or maybe a mug warmer, since there was a wire coming out the back of it.

Jay snatched up the glass, putting her phone in its place, glancing at her laptop screen in the process. "Hey, what is that, a dating site?"

"Yeah."

He frowned. Mack didn't know why he would, though. He often encouraged her to be proactive with her love life (or glaring lack thereof). "Any luck?"

"Oh, yeah. Loads," she answered. Even her sarcasm was laced with defeat.

"Do tell." Jay sat down on the couch next to her and got comfortable.

"Well, okay. Let's start with Tom, here." She touched the screen and a picture of a lanky man with poker straight hair cut into a style that had gone out with grunge. "He's employmentally-challenged and looking for a strong woman who's not hung up on stereo typical male-female roles."

"Translation: he's a mooch."

"Bingo. But he's a prince compared to this guy." A swipe of her index finger took her back to a previous profile. Stylishly-short blonde hair hung artfully over the left side of his forehead, stopping just above mossy colored eyes so green they had to have been Photoshopped.

"This is Chad. He was captain of his high-school gymnastics team, and proudly counts himself among the gifted one percent of the human male population that is sufficiently well-endowed and flexible enough to suck his own dick."

"Lucky bastard," Jay murmured. "What does he need a woman for?"

"My thoughts exactly."

"That's all you got?"

"Nope, one more." She tapped the tablet and brought up a clean-cut, nondescript guy with dirty blonde hair, medium brown eyes, and an awkward, forced,   really-hate-having-my-picture-taken constipated smile.

"He doesn't seem too bad," Jay said charitably, tilting his head one way and then the other, as if that would make the image better.

"He kind of looks like a douche, don't you think?"

"Maybe that's just his resting douche face."

"His what?"

"Resting douche face. It's like a resting bitch face – you know, when a woman looks like a total bitch even when she's completely chill? Except this is for guys who are actually really nice and just have the bad luck to look like a douche."

Mack considered this briefly. "Or he really is a total douche." She squinted at the accompanying bio. "He's forty-two, a tax accountant, and still lives with his mother."

"Jesus, why would you put something like that on your profile?" Jay shook his head in disbelief. "It makes you wonder what he's not telling you. Seriously, Mack. Why are you even looking at this crap? You can do so much better than this."

Mack closed down the site with a heavy sigh. "Yeah, they're beating down the doors."

He patted his leg in invitation. After only a moment's hesitation, she set aside her laptop and crawled into his lap. His sculpted arms wrapped around and held her. Jay was the only one she allowed to see her weakness. The only one she trusted enough.

"What about the detective?"

She shrugged. "We went for coffee."

"And?"

"It was nice. But then he said he'd call and didn't."

"Maybe he's been busy."

"I'm sure he has," she agreed. "But before we went for coffee, we'd run into each other nearly every day, you know? I even had this crazy idea that he might be seeking me out."

"And now?"

"Nothing. Nada. Zip."

That heaviness in her chest intensified. Why couldn't she find someone who liked her for who she was? She was a good person, or at least tried to be. She wasn't Dee, but she wasn't exactly hideous, either.

"Have you tried texting him? Maybe doing a little path-crossing of your own?"

She shook her head. This was one instance where she didn't want to take the lead.

Her mind went back to their last heart-to-heart, when Jay had suggested she embrace her femininity more. She'd been thinking a lot about that over the last couple days, especially since being around Nick had made her feel more like a woman than she had in a long time.

Her conclusion? Maybe Jay had a point. Maybe she just needed to rewrap the package a little. Get someone interested enough to take a closer look and see something more than the cocky smartass she showed the world. To see that beneath the tough outer shell was a woman.

The more she thought about it, the more she was convinced that if she wanted things to change, she had to be willing to change a little, too. She could do that, right? She was a United States Marine, goddammit. She could do anything she set her mind to.

It wouldn't have to be anything too drastic. A few baby steps, just to see what happened. Inside, she would still be her. It wasn't as if she was completely selling out.

"Jay?"

"Yeah, baby girl?"

"Can we call Marcus?"

Jay pulled away enough to look in her eyes for several long moments, then gave her a squeeze. "You sure?"

"Yeah," she said with more conviction. "I'm sure."

Chapter Twenty-One

~ *Nick* ~

The past week had been a busy one. Nick had stayed at the hospital with Jesse and his mom after spotting a Necromancer skulking around the ER. The guy wasn't one of the major players, just a low-level wannabe trying to work his way up. Didn't matter. Nick had memorized the face and bios of all of them.

As soon as the doctor released Jesse the next morning, Nick picked up the supplies Gail had ready and drove Jesse and his mom up to Sam's cabin. It really was 'God's country' up there, and probably the safest place for them until things calmed down. He got them settled in and ensured they had everything they needed before heading back to Covendale.

On his way, all he could think of was how much Mack would enjoy the area. Big, tall trees filtered the sun into dappling shafts of light.

Varying shades of green stretched out as far as the eye could see. Stunning vistas appeared and re-appeared as he worked his way up and down the mountains. During their conversation at Ground Zero, Mack had mentioned several times that she liked the outdoors. Perhaps, if things continued to go well, he'd suggest a brief getaway. They could go hiking. Camp out under the open skies. Maybe share a sleeping bag...

He cooled those thoughts when his pants grew uncomfortably tight. As much as he wanted to know how far her voice would carry as he made her scream in pleasure, he wouldn't rush things. He wanted more than just her naked body beneath, above, and beside him; he wanted to see her smile. Hear her laugh. Feel her hand in his as they discovered things together.

It was scary stuff for a guy who'd only recently decided to move forward with his life.

Which was yet another reason for him to take it slow and let things move forward at a natural pace. It would give him time to find his footing, and give them both a chance to get to know each other better and build a solid foundation.

It had been a couple days since their coffee date. Nick figured enough time had passed for him to contact her and ask her out again without seeming too eager.

Or desperate.

With luck, she'd agree to another coffee date, or maybe more. Was it too soon to ask her to dinner, maybe a movie? Nick decided that after getting some much-needed sleep, he'd grab a quick shower and shave and head over to *Seize* to get his Mack fix and play it by ear.

Unfortunately, things didn't quite work out that way.

When Nick got to the precinct to give his report to the chief, he learned that Jesse's house had been hit. Thankfully, uniformed patrols had been keeping an eye on the place and managed to apprehend those responsible: two guys, both affiliated with the Necromancers MC.

Once again putting his plans on hold, Nick spent as much time as possible trying to get information from them before they lawyered up. One of the guys was in his late-twenties, heavily tatted, pierced, and muscled. He had a rap sheet a mile long. Unsurprisingly, he had nothing to say.

The other guy was younger, barely out of high school. He acted tough, too, but he hadn't been tempered the same way his buddy had. He hadn't done hard time outside of a few stints in juvie. Nick concentrated his efforts on him. He didn't get much, but what he did get was a possible lead on 'Zeke'.

By the time he was finished, Nick was running on fumes. As much as he wanted to see Mack, he needed a few hours of sleep and some food first. Bleary-eyed, Nick fired off a quick text to Mack and crashed.

He'd only intended to sleep for a few hours, but when he woke up, it was morning. The first thing he did was check his phone to see if Mack had responded. There was a reply, but it wasn't the one he'd hoped for: *No, you can't see me tonight, asshat. I'm busy. And you're not my type.*

Nick groaned and palmed his face. Apparently, he'd texted his old partner, Max, instead of Mack.

Sorry, not meant for you. Nick tapped out the text and hit send, then retyped the original message and sent that, confirming that this time, he sent it to the right number.

Nick's phone rang as he was shaving. It wasn't Mack, but Max. "Missing me, huh?"

"Like I said, not for you."

A deep, rumbling laugh. "So you said. Got yourself a woman already, huh?"

Nick smiled, imagining Mack's reaction to being called 'his woman'. "I'm working on it."

"Good for you, man. Listen, I was going to call you anyway. I got some information on that MC you were asking about. Word on the street is that the club is ramping up their activity on the east coast. They hit up these small-town chapters as suppliers to the locals, absorb them into the bigger organization behind the scenes, and hook them up to the bigger network — for a percentage, of course."

"Any idea who's running the expansion?"

"Nothing definite, but it's big enough that it's in the DEA's crosshairs. Sounds like what you're dealing with is right up their alley. You might want to give them a call."

"Got a name?"

"Yeah. Special Agent Greg Bartholomew is the one taking the lead on this." Max rattled off the number.

"Thanks, Max."

"Anytime. And hey, good luck."

After hanging up, Nick considered texting Max again, then decided against it. He needed to see her instead.

It seemed as if the universe was conspiring against him, though. He went into the station house first and filled the chief in on what he'd learned, then put in a call to Special Agent Bartholomew. While he was waiting for the agent to return his call, he took care of the small mountain of to-do's that had accumulated in his short absence.

It was late afternoon before he made it over to *Seize*. It didn't take him long to find Mack, but once he did, he had to blink several times. She didn't just look good. She looked *amazing*.

The changes were subtle, but there nonetheless. Her ponytail was about two inches shorter and sported streaks of light and dark that hadn't been there before. Her skin practically glowed with radiance.

Her clothes were different, too. Still workout appropriate, but sexier. Dare he hope that he might be part of the motivation behind the changes?

Mack hadn't noticed him yet. He watched, transfixed, as she moved over toward the rack of silver and black hand weights. He wasn't the only one. Plenty of other male (and some female) eyes were looking her way, too. An irrational surge of jealousy rose up inside him.

Chapter Twenty-Two

~ *Mack* ~

"What!?" she asked Kent irritably, letting her voice convey the annoyance she felt at being so openly ogled. But she was kind of pleased, too.

She lowered the weights and reached for her water. Detective Kent Emerson was one of the hottest guys in the gym. Lean, roped muscle, bronze skin, and penetrating blue eyes. His sandy blonde hair always looked as if a woman had been running her fingers through it just moments earlier — and probably had, if the rumors were true.

Mack had never been particularly drawn to him, but they got along well enough. The man was serious about his personal fitness and generally friendly. He wasn't Nick, but he wasn't exactly dog food, either.

"You look different, Mack."

He studied her as if she was one of those "I Spy" picture books, looking for hidden things. She almost laughed at the serious concentration in his expression, biting her tongue to keep from telling him not to strain himself. One of the things Jay told her was that her blunt, often colorful utterances were red flags to a guy who might otherwise be interested, and that she should practice verbal restraint, at least at first.

"You did something with your hair," he said finally.

She arched a brow, neither confirming nor denying his guess. She had, in fact, had it cut into soft layers. She had even allowed Marcus to add some subtle highlights and lowlights. And the fifty-dollar shampoo and crème rinse she'd used that morning really did make her hair look shiny and healthy and smell rather exotic.

His eyes travelled down the length of her body and back up again, his gaze not lewd, exactly, but appreciative and assessing. She was wearing the same workout clothes she always did ... sort of.

Mack bit back a smile, sensing the wheels turning in his head. Yes, her shorts and tank were the same color and general style, but instead of being genuine military-issue, this outfit came from a designer and was a size smaller than she normally wore. The snug shorts and subtly-fitted T made the most of her toned assets.

She had also spent a good part of her free time in her bathroom with an all-over depilatory crème, pumice stone, and a moisturizing bronzer. As a result, her skin was smooth, sleek, and glowing, and not because she'd just run five miles on the treadmill.

Too bad the wrong detective was noticing.

"Something you wanted to say, Kent?" she asked, hands on hips, drawing his attention from where they'd stalled briefly on her breasts back down. Hips that looked damned good, if she did say so herself.

"Uh, yeah," he said, his Adam's apple visibly bobbing. His voice sounded a little rougher than usual. Mack's confidence grew.

Kent shifted his weight to his back foot, using the small towel he had wrapped around his neck to wipe some of the sweat coursing in rivulets down from his neck and into his muscle tank. Without conscious thought, Mack's eyes followed the movement.

"Do you have a date for Friday?"

Her eyes snapped up to his. "Excuse me?"

"A date. For Friday. You know, the big shindig?"

"Oh, right," she said, averting her eyes. Every year the town hosted a community ball. Everything was donated by local businesses, from the decorated hall to the sumptuous food. Tickets were a bit pricey at a hundred dollars each, but all proceeds were split among local charities. Mack bought a ticket, as always, but had no intention of going. Well, she might have considered it if a certain new-to-town detective was going, but she hadn't seen Nick all week.

"You *are* going, right?" he pressed.

She shrugged and used a towel to blot the sweat

from her neck, hoping she didn't smell too offensive. Her deodorant soap usually did the job, but she'd gone with the moisturizing body wash and matching scented body mist this morning instead. A discreet sniff assured her she was still fit for being around others. "Wasn't planning on it."

"Why not? Do you have something against having a good time?" His teasing, roguish grin set her just slightly off-balance. She wasn't used to people she didn't know well asking her personal questions. Fitness-related stuff, sure. But this?

"Fancy parties aren't really my thing."

"What exactly is your thing, Mack?" he asked, his eyes twinkling.

Was he *flirting* with her? Men like Kent Emerson didn't flirt with women like her. To them, she was 'one of the guys'. Except Kent's gaze probably didn't surreptitiously scan the length of the other guys' bodies like his was doing to hers at that very moment.

Holy crap. It seemed like Marcus's make-over might have worked a little too well. Was this what it felt like to be Dee?

She couldn't completely stop the blush from rising in her cheeks, cursing her body for allowing it to happen. If she was lucky, maybe he'd just think she was flushed from her workout.

Sassy Mack rose up and took over when Girly Mack came close to fluttering her eyes. "Wouldn't you like to know," she smirked instead.

"Yeah, I would," he said, further shocking her.

Kent shifted again, looking less smug and more

uncertain than he had only moments earlier. His eyes flicked away, as if he'd just admitted something he shouldn't have. Mack followed his eyes, saw a couple of his buddies looking their way. "How about going with me on Friday?"

She blinked, keeping her expression neutral while her heart thundered inside the walls of her chest. Surely, she had misheard. "Are you asking me on a date, Kent?"

"Yeah, I guess I am."

"Why?" she asked before she could stop herself.

"Jesus, Mack," he laughed somewhat uncertainly, shaking his head. "I should have known you wouldn't make this easy." When she continued to stare at him, he gave her a crooked smile. "All right. You're not like everyone else, okay? I'm intrigued. I want to know more about you, other than the fact that you can kick the ass of pretty much everyone in here, including me."

Mack didn't know what to say to that. Was he kidding? She stared up at him, waiting for the 'Ha! Gotcha!' or the 'I'm just messing with you, Mack' that, after one really long, awkward silence, didn't come.

Kent was the first to break eye contact. "You know what? Forget it. I'm sorry I—"

"Okay," she said quickly.

"What?"

"I said okay. I'll go with you on Friday."

Surprise etched his features before turning into a grin. "All right then. Pick you up at seven?"

She nodded. "Sure."

Mack grabbed her towel and made her way to the locker room, shocked by the events of the last few minutes. What the hell had she just gotten herself into?

Chapter Twenty-Three

~ Nick ~

Nick watched the exchange from across the room. What the hell was Emerson up to? Just last week he'd been bragging to anyone who'd listen how he'd hooked up with Delilah.

Nick didn't care about that. In fact, he thought Kent and Delilah were perfect for each other. What he *did* care about was the way the guy had been looking at Mack.

And about whatever he had said to make Mack go all deer-in-the-headlights like that.

She looked good today, even better than usual, and he wasn't the only one who noticed. Guys who normally wouldn't have given her a second glance now couldn't seem to take their eyes off of her.

"What are you looking so smug about, Emerson?" Nick asked, walking over to where the other detective was now knuckle-bumping a few of his buddies.

"Kent just asked Mack out," said one of the other guys with a look of awe on his face.

"And she accepted," said another.

Nick kept his features carefully neutral, despite the fist clenching around his intestines and twisting. "I didn't know you had a thing for Mack."

Kent grinned back at him, too arrogantly to mean anything good.

"Kent's going where no man has gone before," his buddy joked. "Dude, you are the master. I can't believe you are going to get a piece of that."

A deadly combination of disgust, rage, and jealousy washed over Nick. He didn't like them talking about Mack that way. Forcing his fists to unclench before anyone noticed, he said, "I take it Mack doesn't usually date guys from the gym?"

A dark-haired guy named Zane looked surprised at his question. "You're new here, so you wouldn't know."

"Wouldn't know what?"

"Mack doesn't date *anybody*, man. We all kind of figured she was, well, you know…"

"No, I don't know," Nick said with a tight smile. "Why don't you explain it to me?"

"Come on, Benning. She was in the service. Runs a gym. Never see her with a guy, other than that gay dude she lives with. Do the math."

Nick did do the math, and the numbers just weren't adding up. "So if you are so certain she prefers women, why ask her out? I mean, Emerson *is* pretty, but still."

Rather than be offended, Kent laughed and

slapped his shoulder. "You're all right, Benning." Without answering his question, Emerson and his buddies headed for the locker room, leaving Nick with a bad feeling in his gut.

Something wasn't right. What the hell had happened while he'd been away? Just a few nights ago, he'd been feeling really good about this thing with Mack. Now she was going to a public event with Emerson?

Instead of seeking out Mack like he'd intended, Nick left shortly afterward and went to pick up his own ticket to the charity ball.

Chapter Twenty-Four

~ *Mack* ~

Mack felt nervous being so far out of her element, but she tried to overcome that. She was here, amidst the beautiful people, just like Cinderella. Her dress wasn't an exclusive designer, and her jewelry was not from Tiffany or Cartier, but they were good pieces. Things her mother said no woman should ever be without – diamonds, gold, and pearls. She had that covered, at least. She wore small but perfect pearl studs and delicate hanging diamond earrings in her doubly-pierced lobes, along with a matching fine gold chain with a pearl in the center and flanked by tiny diamonds. Jay and Marcus had spent hours picking out the perfect dress and accessories, doing her hair and make-up. Mack felt… feminine.

Surprisingly, it wasn't horrible.

Even her date was turning out better than

expected. Kent had picked her up, held the door open for her, and had been a perfect gentleman. It wasn't easy for him, she knew. She caught his buddies snickering more than once. Mack raised her chin, determined not to embarrass him by flipping them off or beating the crap out of those losers.

Mack shifted nervously, her eyes scanning the room as she sipped the glass of white wine Kent had procured for her. A lot of people she recognized from the gym. It was both odd and interesting to see them all dressed up. Her eye automatically sought out Nick Benning, looking especially hot in a traditional black tux. A pang went through her. He appeared to be alone. A couple of times, she could have sworn she felt his eyes on her, but each time she faced him, his attention was elsewhere.

Not for the first time, she wondered if she had said or done something wrong. She'd had such a good feeling after their coffee shop date, but now he seemed determined to avoid her, and her pride wouldn't allow her to walk up to him and ask. Nick had no problem approaching her before, which meant that he should have been able to do so now — assuming he wanted to.

Unless, of course, he was keeping his distance because she was here with Kent. Was it possible that he was jealous? It was a heady, wishful thought, but he had nothing to be jealous of. Kent was nice and he was handsome, but Mack felt none of the tingles she had around Nick. They were simply here as friendly acquaintances, nothing more.

More importantly, if *Nick* had asked her to go to the ball — or for coffee or some Netflix, for that matter — she wouldn't be there with Kent.

"Would you like to get some fresh air?" Kent asked, his hand lightly resting on her lower back. The innocuous contact felt strange, but since his hand wasn't wandering any farther south, she didn't want to make a big deal over it.

"Yes, please," she said honestly.

"You look stunning tonight, Mack," he complimented as he led her out into the cool evening air. It felt wonderful after the heat of the crowded room and she inhaled deeply, filling her lungs. The local florist had gone all out with her donation, filling the landscaped patio with dozens of fragrant potted gardenias and freshly cut pine boughs.

"Thanks," she said, feeling the blush rise in her cheeks. Had any man ever called her stunning before?

He shifted his weight as though he was experiencing a slight case of the awkwards, too, and Mack couldn't help but feel flattered by that. She'd made men nervous before, but for totally different reasons. Never because someone thought she looked *stunning*.

"I mean," he said, waving his hand, "who knew you were hiding all that?"

Mack's blush deepened. Her first covert foray into Victoria's Secret was proving to be well worth it. The barely-there thong did make her butt look amazing through the clingy material, and the lacy push-up bra accentuated full breasts that were normally smushed and flattened by her preferred athletic sportswear.

How would a confident, desirable woman respond to something like that? Mack tried to imagine what Dee would say. "Glad you like it," she murmured.

Apparently, he did, because seconds later, he was pressing her against the red brick wall and trying to snake her internal plumbing by sticking his tongue down her throat. Caught off guard, her hand-to-hand training kicked in automatically, and a moment later, he was wheezing on the ground in the fetal position, clutching his family jewels.

"What the fuck?!" he ground out around the moan.

Mortified, Mack dropped to her knees and reached out for him. "Oh, crap. I am so sorry. It was instinct. I panicked."

"Get away from me!" He recoiled from her touch. Another apology was on her lips when his eyes glanced toward the open patio doors. "You win!"

Mack turned around to see Dee smiling broadly. Some of Kent's friends crowded around, looking uncomfortable. She looked back to her date, who no longer looked anything like a gentleman. "This was a *game*?"

Kent didn't meet her eyes. He didn't have to.

"More like a challenge," Dee said smugly, looking at her nails before smirking at Mack triumphantly.

"A challenge," Mack repeated softly. "What kind of challenge?"

"Yes. Kent fashions himself as somewhat of a ladies' man. So much, in fact, that he could even convert those who, shall we say, don't swing that way? I simply suggested he put his money where his mouth is." She grinned wickedly. "Looks like I won."

Mack rose slowly to her feet. It all made perfect sense now. How could she have been so stupid? Dee hadn't changed. She was still the cruel, evil creature she'd always been, lashing out when she didn't get her way. Even worse, this wasn't the first time Dee had tried something like this. Back in high school though, Mack had been smart enough *not* to accept the quarterback's invitation to the spring dance.

Mack summoned her courage and her dignity and looked down at Kent, who was still clutching his family jewels and irrationally, felt a stab of pity for him.

"What did you win? A night between Delilah's legs? The joke's on you, pal. She gives that shit away for free."

"Jesus, Mack," he wheezed. "It was all in fun, you know?"

"Yeah. It's been a real blast. Excuse me," she said politely. The wall of men blocking the doorway parted. She paused, fighting the urge to wipe that smug smirk off of Dee's face and said quietly, "Find another place to live."

The flash in Delilah's eyes was satisfying. Even more satisfying, in a few hours, when Dee tried to return to the house and found her bags packed and on the porch, and the security codes changed, the reality of her situation would sink in.

Her father wanted Princess Dee to learn responsibility? Well, Dee had just been placed in the accelerated program.

Mack kept her eyes forward and her head held high as she crossed the dance floor toward the main entrance. Judging by the number of curious eyes turned her way as she made her way across the floor, Dee's "challenge" hadn't been a secret.

Mack refused to acknowledge any of them. Once outside the hotel, she pulled off her heels and rapped on the window of the town's only cab. As she slipped into the back seat, she thought she heard someone calling her name.

She ignored it, refusing to acknowledge the emotions trying to take hold. She'd deal with those later. Right now, she was in full-on mission mode, creating a mental list of things she needed to do. Giving the driver her address, she sank back into the seat and closed her eyes.

The house was dark when she got there, and Mack was glad for it. She hurriedly stripped out of her dress and went into the bathroom. The pretty woman looking back at her with smoky eyes and stained lips was a stranger. Mack scrubbed the make-up from her face vigorously and brushed out the curls that had taken nearly an hour to create, pulling it all back in a tight ponytail.

She looked again and nodded in approval. *This* was who she was.

Her phone vibrated again; Jay's name displayed on the screen. She knew it wouldn't have taken long for word to get back to him; the whole place was probably buzzing, having a good laugh at her expense.

Jay and Marcus had been at the event, too, but she didn't believe for a minute he had known. He would have found some way to warn her, or better yet, turn the tables. The last thing she wanted was for him – for anyone – to see her when her emotions were running so close to the surface. She needed a few hours to get her shit together before she did that.

Mack grabbed some garbage bags and went to the guest bathroom. One swipe of her arm was all it took to clear the vanity. A couple of armloads and the contents of the guest closet were gone as well. Feeling a bit like the Grinch, she grinned in satisfaction as she tossed bag after bag to the curb.

Then she went back into the house and reset the security codes, firing off a quick text to Jay with the new numbers. She pulled on cargos, thick socks, and a couple pieces of comfortable, wicking base layers and flannel, then packed her rucksack with the efficiency of a seasoned Marine. Within ten minutes of entering the house, she was leaving it again.

She hopped in her Jeep Renegade and drove up to the state game lands before locking it up and proceeding on foot. Only when she paused at the rock outcropping did she pull out her phone and thumb a quick text to Jay. Judging by the number of texts he'd send in the last thirty minutes, he was worried.

Jay: *Where are you?*

Jay: *Check in, Marine.*

Jay: *Seriously, Mack, where TF are you?*

Jay: *Nice lawn decorations, btw.*

She snorted, deleting texts sent by anyone other than him; everyone else could go screw themselves as far as she was concerned.

Mack: *I'm okay. Really. Back tomorrow, Sunday at the latest. Namaste.*

Then she turned off her phone, slipped it into the bottom of her pack, and continued up the rock face.

Chapter Twenty-Five

~ *Nick* ~

Nick watched the cab drive away with Mack inside. He'd called out to her as she'd stormed by but she hadn't even looked his way. Something, or rather some*one*, had upset her enough to leave, and he had a good idea who that someone was.

He turned on his heel and went back into the venue. It had been hard enough watching Mack arrive on Emerson's arm. God, she'd looked fantastic. Classy and feminine and so damn sexy that she'd had every set of male eyes on her the moment she'd walked in. Powerful, possessive caveman urges had risen up, making him want to march right over there, toss her over his shoulder, and take her into a utility closet until the only man on her mind was *him*.

Instead, he'd ordered a double and stepped outside until he could get his inner caveman under control. Now, however, a different urge gripped him. The need to protect and avenge.

Finding out what happened — the gist of it anyway — hadn't taken long. Rumors were already running rampant, as was the cracking buzz of electricity in the crowd that came with them.

Nick mentally kicked himself for not doing something earlier. His gut had told him that something wasn't quite right about Emerson's sudden interest in Mack. Now, as he looked across the room and saw Delilah staring back at him with a smug smile, he couldn't believe he hadn't seen it. Delilah *was* a lot like Eve Sanderson — a spoiled, manipulative, vengeful creature who used others to get what she wanted and apparently, Emerson was her latest tool.

A familiar rage simmered below the surface. No one deserved to be on the receiving end of that kind of malice. Certainly not Mack, who, for as tough as she was on the outside, was a kind, generous, and caring woman on the inside.

He stalked across the room. Judging by the way Emerson was hunched over and pale, he'd taken a shot to the jewels. Good. The guy was on his feet, which meant Nick felt no qualms about hauling back and punching Emerson right in the face.

Emerson dropped like a stone. "What the fuck was that for?" he railed, his hands moving from his groin to his nose.

"Because I can't hit *her*," Nick said, glaring at

Delilah. Her eyes flashed. The bitch was actually enjoying the show.

Emerson scowled, then nodded. "Point taken."

Nick reached out a hand and hauled Emerson to his feet. "What did Mack ever do to you, anyway?"

"Nothing," Emerson admitted.

"I hope she—" Nick glanced sideways at Delilah, whose lips were now formed into a scowling pout "—was worth it. And that *you* are going to offer your heartfelt and sincere apologies to Mack the first chance you get."

Nick left without waiting for a response, pulling out his cell phone and tapping as he went.

He put some of the blame upon himself. He should have asked Mack to the ball, or better yet, just donated the money and taken them out someplace they both would have enjoyed more than this dog and pony pageant. Maybe then she wouldn't have agreed to go with that douchebag, and she sure as hell wouldn't have left feeling like anything less than the amazing woman she was.

He'd seen the flyers around town, heard people talking about it, but the thought that Mack might want to attend a formal ball hadn't occurred to him.

He should have listened to his instincts. He'd known from the moment he'd first seen her that she was special. That he wanted something more.

The image of her face just as she left the party haunted him as he made his way across town. Mack had been totally blindsided by Kent's idiocy. The

look on her face as she'd crossed that ballroom…
Jesus.

Well, one thing was for certain. Emerson's stunt had just changed his game plan dramatically, and Nick was no longer content to stand on the sidelines and watch.

He was putting himself into the game.

He'd no sooner slipped his phone back into his pocket than it started vibrating. Pulling it out, he held it up to his ear. "Mack, where are you?"

There was a long moment of silence, then a feminine voice came through the tiny speaker. "Is this Nick Benning?"

It had been years, but he would have recognized her voice anywhere. "Liz?"

"Yes! Is it true? You're really in Covendale?"

"Yeah."

"Listen, we're on our way home. Don't go anywhere until I get there, okay?"

Nick almost smiled at the big sister bossiness in her tone. "I'm not going anywhere, Liz."

Chapter Twenty-Six

~ *Mack* ~

One of the reasons Mack moved to Pennsylvania was because she'd fallen in love with the mountains. They weren't the biggest, or the most well-known, but they were some of the prettiest and least spoiled she'd seen. Being here reminded her of the times she used to go hiking with her father, before his inventions were patented, before he became a self-made multimillionaire.

Life had been so much simpler then. In preparation for their adventures, her mom would make them ham and cheese sandwiches, and her dad would fashion walking sticks out of branches that had fallen from the stoic, centuries old maple trees in their backyard. Then, with their wrapped sandwiches safely tucked into her Nickelodeon-themed lunch box and a couple of juice boxes in her father's knapsack, they'd go exploring.

They never went very far, she realized much later, but to her younger self, it seemed as if they had. He taught her all about different kinds of trees and plants, what was safe to eat and what to avoid. She learned how to read animal tracks and scat, how to fashion a splint from sticks, how to tell time by looking at the sky and gauge the approach of a storm by watching the trees and listening to the animals.

When they'd find the perfect spot, they'd make a small fire and roast their ham and cheese sandwiches on y-shaped sticks and talk until the sun started going down and it was time to head back home. Her mom would be waiting for them on the back porch, gently rocking back and forth on the swing her dad had put up for her on Mother's Day…

Those were the things she thought about as she climbed higher and put more distance between her and the rest of the world; that's where her love for the great outdoors had been born. Away from civilization, that connection to something much larger gave her the focus she needed.

When her lungs were burning and her legs were screaming, she found herself a cozy spot to make camp. She filled her canteen from the nearby stream, gathered some dry kindling, and dug a pit for a small fire. Once she'd ringed the hole with rocks and set up her wood in the shape of a teepee, she lit a tiny blaze and used some pine needles to create a soft base for her sleeping bag. Only then did she pause and allow herself to process the events of the evening.

Tears fell silently for a few minutes, the only ones she would shed. She had gotten nothing less than she deserved, a just punishment for trying to be something she was not. *Be true to yourself.* Maybe she should have that embroidered on a pillow. Better yet, she should have that tattooed on her body where she could look at it often and remind herself of the wisdom in those four little words. Yeah, when she got back, she was definitely going to pay a visit to the ink shop over in Birch Falls and have Tiny, the local tattoo artist and master inker, sketch something out.

Having made that decision (a plan that involved doing something always helped), she settled back and tried to relax. She took deep, cleansing breaths, filling her lungs with the crisp, clean mountain air. A sense of awe filled her at the sight of the perfect velvety canvas above, the expanse of deep midnight blue-black serving as a reminder of just how small she and her problems were in the overall scheme of things. She needed this, needed the time and the perspective to heal her bruised heart.

No, that wasn't quite right, she realized with startling clarity. It was her *pride* that had been damaged, not her heart, because she really didn't have feelings for Kent beyond a superficial kind of friendship, one based more in business and convenience. He was an acquaintance, nothing more.

That little epiphany made it a bit easier to take the next breath. Pride wasn't all that important in the overall scheme of things. She was still *Mack*, still whole. Her heart was still intact, and that's what really mattered.

Now if it had been Nick instead of Kent... well, that *would* have really hurt. But thank God no one knew that, not even Jay, and Mack was going to make damn sure it stayed that way. Her feelings for Nick were her dirty little secret, and if no one knew, then no one could use them against her.

Tonight and maybe tomorrow night, she would recharge under the moon and stars. Then she would head back to town, refreshed and ready to kick some serious ass.

Chapter Twenty-Seven

~ *Nick* ~

Nick kept running long past his usual five miles. He'd been out early, too many things on his mind to take advantage of the fact that it was a Sunday and he could sleep in. He still had some things he wanted to pull together for his upcoming call with the DEA agent. He was heading over to his sister's later that afternoon. And Mack was still MIA. Jay had told him that Mack was off rusticating, whatever the hell that meant, and that she'd be back when she was ready.

In the meantime, he was forced to bide his time. He'd already decided that he was going to stop pussyfooting around and let Mack know how he felt. They could take it slow, take it fast, or somewhere in between, as long as they took it together.

Unless, of course, she told him pointblank to

fuck off.

If that turned out to be the case, he'd respect her wishes. That didn't mean he'd give up easily. There was too much potential there, too much electricity crackling between them whenever they were in the same room. She'd felt it too, he was sure of it. It was in the way her eyes softened when she looked at him. In the sound of her laugh on those rare occasions when those walls she surrounded herself with became a little less solid.

Now, thanks to her sister's mean-spirited stunt and Emerson thinking more with his dick than his head, Nick was going to have to work even harder to convince Mack that his motive was pure and his intentions honorable. It wasn't going to be easy. Good thing he was a determined, patient man. Deep in his gut, he knew he and Mack could be so good together.

Now he just needed to convince *her*.

Knowing Mack wasn't at *Seize*, Nick had opted to go for a run along some of the local trails instead. It was a nice day and the cool, fresh morning air helped clear his thoughts. Running outside also had the added benefit of reducing the chances he'd run into someone he *didn't* care to see. Every time he thought about the smirk on Delilah's face, the anger began to simmer all over again.

He paused at a crossroads and checked his phone. Still no response from Mack.

Nick turned left and headed toward the river

trail. Where was she? Was she alone? Was she okay? He didn't worry so much for her safety; he believed Mack was more than capable of taking care of herself. In fact, Mack was probably the most capable woman he knew. But even strong people sometimes needed someone to fall into. He should know. He'd lived as an island for almost ten years.

Forcing worries for Mack toward the back of his mind, he focused his attention on other things, like the fact that in a few hours, he was going to be seeing Liz again and meeting her husband.

He wasn't sure how he felt about that. After his encounter with Brandon Grayson, Nick had done some information gathering, a process which may or may not have included background checks on Miles Grayson, his brother, and his son, all of whom now resided in Covendale. Some of the things he'd found had been surprising, to say the least.

For instance, Adam Grayson, Miles's younger brother, had been the one responsible for finally putting Eve Sanderson away. Adam had been a victim of Eve's warped obsession, just as he had been all those years ago.

Not for the first time, Nick wished he'd known enough to have his blood tested when he'd woken up dazed and confused after only having a few beers. Fresh out of college, he didn't have the resources or experience to suspect what had happened to him. Girls were often warned about the dangers of someone slipping something into their drinks at a party, but that wasn't something most guys thought could happen to them.

Of course, he hadn't been in his right mind then, either, having just discovered that he'd lost his Annie. By the time they'd put all the tragic pieces together, it had been too late to prove anything, and with the power the Sandersons wielded in the local community, unsubstantiated claims from a man half out of his mind with grief and guilt hadn't been taken seriously.

Thankfully, times were changing, and Adam Grayson had been able to do what Nick (and who knew how many others?) hadn't.

As for Miles Grayson, well, he had been some hot shot marketing representative. From what Nick managed to dig up, after divorcing his first wife, Grayson had been somewhat of a playboy, pulling in big bucks in sales and marketing and jet-setting around the world. Then one day, he just walked away from it all, enrolled in the architecture program at the local university, and joined his brother's construction company doing manual labor. Was it a mid-life crisis, or the actions of a man who'd finally found what he'd been looking for? For Liz's sake, Nick sincerely hoped it was the latter.

Not leaving any stone unturned, Nick had also researched Miles's ex-wife, looking for any red flags that might indicate a history of abuse or domestic violence. Thankfully, he found none. Liz might be the older sibling, but that didn't mean Nick's protective brotherly instincts didn't still kick in.

A dull ache radiated across his chest, one that had nothing to do with the grueling pace he'd set for himself. This one came from guilt and regret. He shouldn't have waited so long to come home. He should have been there for Liz, watching out for her the way brothers were supposed to look out for their sisters, meeting boyfriends and vetting would-be suitors.

He should have been helping with his parents, too, instead of leaving Liz to handle all that. After speaking with Liz the night before, Nick had called them. His mother had been surprised to hear from him and absolutely thrilled when he'd told her he was moving back to Covendale permanently. His father didn't seem to remember that he'd ever left.

That was another thing he and Liz were going to talk about. At one point she had hinted that their father was showing signs of Alzheimer's, but Nick had no idea things had progressed quite so far. As soon as things settled down a bit, Nick was going to fly down to Florida for a long overdue visit. Or maybe he'd offer to fly them up. Autumn wasn't too far away, and his mother always said how much she loved the colorful, changing foliage. Then he could introduce them to Mack…

…And just like that, his thoughts were back on

Mack.

He checked his phone again. Still nothing.

He shook his head and picked up the pace, heading back towards his place where he checked his phone again. And again after he took a shower. And after he dressed and poured himself another cup of coffee.

Refusing to call Jay again, Nick set the mug beside him as he compiled more info on the Necromancers. All the interviewing and digging he'd done was finally beginning to pay off. A local hierarchy was emerging, one that would prove extremely useful to Special Agent Bartholomew and his team. Nick had spoken to Bartholomew several times over the past week, and after each conversation, it became clearer that the Covendale-based MC was just the tip of a very dirty iceberg.

His cell phone remained silent until it was time for him to leave for Liz's. With a heavy sigh, Nick grabbed the mobile and slipped it into his pocket.

Liz had the door open before he even got out of the car. Any concerns he had about Liz not being happy to see him vanished the instantly she wrapped her arms around his neck and hugged him hard right there in the driveway.

"I can't believe it," she said with tears in her eyes as she stepped back and looked at him. "My baby brother is all grown-up."

He laughed. He'd been in his early twenties when he'd left, hardly a kid, though admittedly, he had bulked up a bit since then. A few years picking up work as a ranch hand, then the academy, had broadened his shoulders and hardened his body.

Liz had changed too. She'd always been slim and feminine, but she was even more so now. Time had only enhanced her natural beauty and the sheer happiness that radiated from her made her glow with health and vitality.

"And look at you! No one is ever going to believe you're older than me."

A tall, dark man watched the exchange from the doorway, amusement lighting his eyes. Nick recognized the man instantly as the one he'd been cyberstalking.

Liz grabbed his hand as if she was afraid he'd disappear and tugged him toward the condo. "Come on, there's someone I want you to meet. Nick, my husband, Miles. Miles, this is my brother, Nick."

The men shook hands. Miles's grip was firm and strong, his smile warm and friendly. "Nice to meet you, Nick. I've heard a lot about you."

Nick wished he could say the same, but seeing as he hadn't even known his sister had tied the knot until a few weeks ago, he couldn't. Liz must have picked up on the direction of his thoughts because she said, "I wanted to tell you, but I didn't know how to reach you."

Her voice was even, but her eyes couldn't hide the hurt she obviously felt. "I'm so sorry, Liz. I should have done a better job keeping in touch."

"I wish you would have. I didn't know where you were, or even if…" She let the sentence hang, and the guilt weighed even heavier across his shoulders.

"I know. And I am sorry. Here." Nick reached into his pocket and pulled out a small wrapped box. "I know this doesn't make up for things, but…"

"What's this?"

"A present. I missed your birthday this year."

Her eyes misted as she accepted the small package and untied the ribbon. Her small gasp when she saw the crystal wolf made him feel a little better. "I hope you still like Swarovski."

"It's beautiful!" she said between sniffles. "I love it!"

"I'm glad, because I've got nine more in my car, one for every birthday I missed. Every time I moved to a new place, I picked one up."

Liz hugged him again. "I missed you."

"I missed you too, sis."

"We have so much to catch up on."

"Yeah, we do."

Miles held out his hand again. "Nick, it was nice to meet you."

"You're leaving?"

"I have some catching up of my own to do," Miles told him. He kissed Liz on the cheek. "I'll be up at Adam's if you need me."

"Tell Holly I'll call her later."

"Will do."

Liz watched her husband leave, the look of pure love on her face unmistakable. The moment the door closed, she shook her head as if coming out of a trance. "Sorry. That man just does it for me, you know?"

Nick laughed. "Are you happy?"

"So, so happy. Want some coffee?"

"Good. I'd love some. And while we're making it, you can tell me *why you sold my fucking car*."

Sincere regret shone in her eyes. "I'm sorry about that, Nick. I wasn't sure I'd ever see or hear from you again."

"But my *baby*, Liz."

"I know how much you loved that thing but I just couldn't see letting it rot somewhere and I had no way of knowing if you were even *alive* at that point. I thought it would be better to put her in the hands of someone who would care for her as much as you did. And, I didn't *sell* it, I gave it to him for graduation."

Nick was skeptical, finding it hard to believe anyone could care as much about his baby as he had. He'd poured his blood, sweat, and tears into every inch. "And you think that kid will do that?"

"I know he will. He's as much of a gear-head as you were. I know he's dying to talk to you about the Shelby and some of the modifications you made to it. You two are going to get along very well."

"Hmph." Maybe.

Three hours, two cups of coffee, and a slice of

pie later, Liz sat back, shaking her head. "I still can't believe you're actually here."

They'd talked about so much, hitting the highlights of each other's lives over the last ten years. Nick told her how he had wandered around aimlessly before finding a new purpose in law enforcement; Liz told him how she had moved up the ranks in her company, provided an honest, somewhat brutal, update on their parents, and some highlights of her honeymoon travels through the continents.

"You look happy," he commented.

"I am happy," she confirmed. "I mean, don't get me wrong. I was content before, but finding the right one changes everything."

He didn't disagree. Once again, an image of a certain fitness center owner flashed in his mind.

"I want that for you, Nick. And you know what? I think Annie would want you to find someone and be happy, too."

The corner of his mouth tilted. "I just may have, Liz."

Chapter Twenty-Eight

~ *Mack* ~

A few days in the mountains had done wonders, giving her a chance to process and reflect and focus. She'd stayed an extra day and night once Jay had texted her, assuring her that he would take care of everything until she made it back, telling her to take as much time as she needed. Jay always had her back.

She returned stronger than when she'd left. Any self-pity she'd allowed herself was over and done, left behind at a higher elevation where it could burn off with the morning sun. Now she was just pissed. *Really* pissed.

Angry with Delilah. Angry with Kent. Most of all, angry with herself for giving a shit what other people thought of her and trying to live up to a misogynistic society's idea of what a woman *should* be.

Fuck that. And if people didn't like her for who

and what she was, then fuck *them*.

Mack made it back into town around midday. After making a quick stop at the house for a shower and change of clothing, she'd gone right to *Seize*. Thankfully, everything was running smoothly. Her Sunday crew had things well under control. If anyone knew about her Friday night humiliation (and undoubtedly, they did, because Covendale was not a big town), they were smart enough not to say anything to her face.

Satisfied that all was well, she started the second phase of readjusting her attitude. With her iPod turned to the max and her Beats earbuds shoved solidly into her ears, Motley Crue's "Kickstart My Heart" was loud enough to make her brain vibrate. Mack ran full tilt up the graded virtual trail on the treadmill until her heart pounded and sweat dripped from her brow.

Feeling somewhat better, Mack headed down to one of the MMA training rooms and plugged her iPod into the sound system, once again selecting the playlist aptly titled "Kick Ass". Limp Byzkit's "Break Stuff" screamed thru the speakers placed around the room for maximum effect as she bounced on her toes and delivered a dizzying series of jabs, cross-punches, and hooks to the suspended weight bag, listening to the lyrics that so aptly suited her mood. Words that expressed how messed up things could get sometimes, and how it could make you want to lash out and do some damage.

Amen, brother. Sweat poured into her eyes as she spun around and landed a perfectly executed, bone wrenching kick, imagining Kent's head on the padded dummy. Then another. That one was Delilah.

Limp Byzkit segued into Disturbed's "Down with the Sickness." She abandoned the bag and moved to her self-designed mini bodyweight fitness course, created to push her body to its limits, using the beat to pace her chin-ups, push-ups, and sit-ups until her muscles screamed.

Thousand Foot Krutch had her back on the mat, launching into a series of katas choreographed for inflicting maximum pain with an economy of motion to the pounding bass of "Puppet".

"You know, most women cope by taking bubble baths and crying into a tub of Ben and Jerry's."

Jay sat on a stack of workout mats. In the zone, she cast him a glance that would have made anyone else cower, getting only a raised eyebrow in return. Yeah, Jay got it. He knew she wasn't angry with him. He'd seen her raw before, and didn't even flinch now.

"In case you haven't gotten the memo, I'm not most women. As a matter of fact, I understand there's actually a raging debate on whether I was actually born female or was surgically altered later in life."

A combination of disappointment and worry ghosted over his face. "Didn't think you were the type to wallow in self-pity, Mack."

"Thanks for taking care of *Seize*. As for the rest, piss off." She punctuated the statement with a couple of solid hits to the nearby weight bag that had it swinging in a large arc.

"That's more like it," he nodded in approval. "Come on. Hit the showers, Marine."

"What the hell for?"

"Because we're going out. I'm going to get you shitfaced."

Her chest heaved from the exertion as sweat soaked through her clothes. Not the designer ones – those were now in the Goodwill bag, but the ones designed by Uncle Sam. Mack stared at him for long moments. When she grunted and started stalking toward him, he stood up and went into a defensive stance.

Her lips quirked. She must look even fiercer than she'd thought.

"Fine," she said. "But *I* get to pick the place." It sure as hell wasn't going to be one of those pansy-ass clubs with techno pop crap and neon lights and froofy drinks with cute little names. It was going to be dark and dirty and as far from civilized as possible to match her mood. The tranquility of the mountains had given way to the need to cut loose, to free fall into some no holds barred, rip-roaring stress relief. And with Jay there to have her six, she could.

"And we're taking a detour into Birch Falls along the way." Mack didn't stop or vary her path at all, choosing instead to use her shoulder as a battering ram against his right pectoral. Much to his credit, Jay stood his ground and eyed the weight bag - still swinging - and the stuffing spilling out of the

MMA dummy, probably wondering what the hell he had been thinking.

Chapter Twenty-Nine

~ *Nick* ~

Nick looked up at the stage, hardly believing his eyes as a stream of colorful expletives left his lips. Mack was up there, looking like his personal fantasy come to life. She was beyond fierce. Her hair was loose, flowing around her shoulders. Her shirt was gone. Above the camos that sat low on her luscious hips, a hint of six pack abs flashed beneath satiny, tawny skin. And above that, a plain black, front-clasp bra lovingly cupped what were surprisingly full breasts. Her shiny dog tags winked at him from her enticing cleavage as she did lewd — and incredibly hot — gravity defying things to the stripper's pole while a bunch of guys hooted and egged her on.

Gyrating to Hinder's "American Nightmare", slicked with sweat, lost in total abandon, she was the sexiest thing he'd ever seen. And holy hell, was that script a new tat running up the side of her body, covered with clear cling wrap?

"Yeah, that pretty much covers it," Jay agreed, concern etched in his features.

"Explain this to me, Jay."

"Well, Mack was still pretty pissed when I tracked her down and found her kicking the shit out of the equipment. I thought taking her out and having a few drinks, would take her mind off things for a while, you know? Give her a chance to cool down and vent. I didn't expect her to drag me into the tattoo shop and watch while she got those words needled into her skin."

Nick squinted at the calligraphic lettering, but couldn't quite make it out. "What does it say?"

"*Ad te ipso verum est*. It's Latin for 'to thine own self be true'."

Nick nodded. "Go on."

"So then she said she wanted to come here. I've never been in here before but it has a rep for being popular among the armed forces crowd, so I thought she'd be comfortable here, you know?" Jay reached around and put his hand on the back of his neck. "As you can see, it worked."

Nick snorted. Understatement of the year, that.

"Thanks for coming, man."

"No problem," Nick said. When Jay had called earlier and said Mack needed some help, he'd been in the car and on his way before he'd even hung up. He'd never expected this, though. "Did you know she could do this?"

Jay nodded and drank deeply from his beer. "There's not a stripper in the tri-state area that doesn't come to Mack's Booty Camp to get sculpted and into shape."

"*Mack's Booty Camp?*"

"Yeah. I came up with the name. Anyway, the dancers, they *love* her, teach her all the best moves. She practices at the house, says it's like plyometrics, gymnastics, and dance cardio all in one. Never in public, though. She's too self-conscious for that."

Nick looked doubtfully at the stage. That sure as hell didn't look like a woman who had a problem with confidence.

"What did you do to her?" Nick asked. His eyes moved reluctantly away from the stage, taking in the riled-up group of military guys looking hungrily at Mack. That wave of possessiveness started rising up again, and things were going to get real ugly if he didn't do something soon.

"Me? I didn't do anything. I just bought her a few beers. They —" he pointed over toward a table of guys wearing Army tees "– started buying her shots a couple of hours ago." Jay was silent for a couple of moments, then said, "Listen, I'm not sure I did the right thing in calling you. Mack is probably going to flip her shit, so if you want to bail, believe me, I understand."

"Not a chance," Nick told him firmly.

Jay nodded in approval. "I've seen the way you look at her, man."

"Yeah?" he asked, not even bothering to deny it. "How's that?"

"Like she's the one you've been waiting for to

start living again."

Nick smiled, only slightly surprised that Jay had done his homework. Mack was a lucky woman. Everyone should have such fierce friends looking out for them. "You'd make a hell of a detective, Jay. Give me a call if that modelling thing doesn't work out."

Jay laughed. "Yeah, I'll keep that in mind."

"Does Mack know?"

Jay's smile faded. "Oh hell, no. Head in the sand, that one. Plus she's in denial, convinced she's undesirable."

Nick choked. "Are you kidding me?"

"Wish I was. The step-devils must have really done a number on her, and let's face it, most men are intimidated by her awesomeness. Not you, though. I know a man smitten when I see one. And newsflash? Mack murmurs *your* name in her sleep."

Well, *damn*. Nick felt like puffing out his chest and giving it a few solid pounds with alternating fists. "So what's the plan?"

Jay smiled, as if he sensed the surge in Nick' testosterone levels. "Flash that badge and go get your woman. I've got your back."

That sounded like a hell of a plan. Nick made his way over to the edge where Mack was dancing, oblivious to everything except internalizing the rhythm and spirit of Poison's "Unskinny Bop". She looked so damn sexy doing it, too, that he almost let her finish. The problem was, every other male was seeing it, too, and he wanted a private viewing.

It wasn't any of *their* names she murmured in

her sleep.

He reached up and plucked her from the stage, resulting in an instant chorus of boos. Nick didn't hear any of it; he was too preoccupied with the feel of Mack's hot little body tucked into his chest.

It took Mack a few seconds to realize what had happened.

"What the hell, soldier?" she asked, slurring her words slightly as she slid down his body. Her eyes squinted as her head tilted upward toward his face. Her flirty smile faded, turned into genuine confusion. "Nick? What are you doing here?"

"Taking you home."

Her bemusement darkened and she tried to push him away. "Like hell. I'm having fun."

"You're drunk."

"No wonder you made detective," she snickered. "Nothing gets past you." She tried to take a step back and swayed precariously. Thankfully, Jay was there to catch her. "Oh, hey Jay."

"Hey, baby girl." He draped her shirt — the one she'd whipped over her head like a lasso and tossed out to the crowd earlier — over her shoulders.

"Did you call him?" she demanded. Jay nodded. She pinned him with a glare, one that probably would have been far more intimidating if she hadn't been swaying as she did so.

"Come on, Mack. Let's go," Nick said in a low but firm voice as he held on to her arm, wanting to get her out of there before shit really hit the fan. The hairs on the back of his neck were prickling from all of the unhappy looks he was getting from her new admirers.

Mack turned back to Nick, fixing him with her haughty glare. Arousal fired in his veins. She was so unlike any woman he had ever met. Even sloppy drunk and mouthing off she was beautiful.

"Are you arresting me, Detective?" she sneered. "'Cause that is the *only* way I'll ever leave a bar with you."

Arresting her hadn't been his intention, but he could see the merits of the idea. He glanced over her head toward the table of pissed off men now standing, their unhappy eyes focused on him. They were just about to head their way and he was pretty sure it wasn't to buy him a beer.

"So be it." He deftly turned Mack around, pulling both wrists together in one of his large hands as he reached for his cuffs and mechanically began to recite her Miranda rights.

"Jesus," Jay breathed his eyes widening. "Is that really necessary?"

"You can't arrest me!" she spat at him.

"Watch me." One hand pushed against the center of her back, leading her toward the exit.

"What are the charges?" She wriggled in his grasp, trying to use her weight against him. Since he easily had a hundred pounds on her (and wasn't three sheets to the wind), her attempts to escape weren't very effective. It didn't stop her from bringing up her knee in a thrust toward his groin. Nick twisted to the side in time to save his manly bits, which only seemed to piss her off more. She brought her foot up and stomped on his instep — *hard* — then followed up with an attempted head butt (which he mostly deflected).

Nick winced slightly and clenched his teeth. "Let's start with assaulting a police officer and go from there."

The flash of his badge was probably the only thing that kept the angry mob from beating his ass, but he didn't breathe a sigh of relief until Mack was ensconced safely in the back of his car. When he shut the door, she leaned back on the seat and gave it a good solid kick with both feet, hard enough to rock the whole vehicle.

"Don't make me taser you," he warned menacingly. She glared at him, all messy and fired up, cheeks flushed and eyes blazing. Another bolt of lust shot through him. He couldn't help but wonder what that kind of passion would be like if unleashed under other, more appropriate, circumstances. He could almost feel her phantom nails clawing at his back while her powerful thighs wrapped around his hips and she squeezed him with her tight —

"Want me to ride along?" Jay asked, glancing in the back window where Mack was now struggling to sit up and unleashing a torrent of scorching curses, all centered upon exactly what she thought Nick could do with his taser. What *she* would do with it the moment he let his guard down.

"No," Nick exhaled. "I've got this."

"You are either a really brave man or a batshit crazy one."

"Probably a bit of both," Nick said with a wry

smile. Hell, he had to be insane to be thinking the kinds of things he was thinking. The woman was testing every one of his limits and he *liked* it. "Besides. I don't think she's very happy with you right now, either."

Jay turned back to the car, saw the murderous look in her eyes and shuddered. Rubbing the back of his neck, he sighed heavily. "Yeah, good point. It's probably best if she stays out of sight for a while. No need to add more fuel to the fire. Hey, take care of her, will you? She comes off all tough and whatnot, but this …" He shook his head. "Mack doesn't do *this*."

Nick met the other man's eyes and nodded in silent acknowledgement. Jay turned and took a step toward his car, then paused and looked back over his shoulder uncertainly. Nick cast a glance at Mack, who was now looking out of the window in disbelief, her eyes wide with betrayal. "Jay! Don't you leave me, Jay!"

"You know what, Nick? Maybe you should drive my car back. I can take Mack—"

"Go. She'll be fine. I'll take care of her, I promise."

Jay looked at him doubtfully. "You're not really going to taser her, are you?"

Nick's lips twitched. That had been an empty threat. His plans for subduction did not include a taser. "No. Trust me on this, will you?"

By the time Nick manage to convince Jay that Mack would be just fine and slid into the driver's seat, Mack was no longer trying to kick the crap out of his car. She sat perfectly still, as far away from him as physically possible in the cramped space.

"You are a dick," she spit out, drilling holes in the back of his head.

"Sticks and stones, luv," he shot back, affecting his best Jack Sparrow impression as he eased out of the lot. "Seriously, Mack, what the hell were you thinking?"

"What do you care?" He met her eyes in the rearview mirror. She averted them quickly, choosing instead to look out the window.

An excellent question, that. One that he was pretty sure he knew the answer to, but now was not the best time to get into that, or to any of the other hundred or so things he didn't understand. He just knew that his instincts told him he was doing the right thing. "I just do."

"Right. That's why you never called." The words were quiet, but he heard them.

"I had to go out of town on an emergency. And for the record, I *did* text you. You never responded."

She snorted at that, then quieted down. The next time he chanced a glance back, her eyes were closed, her features relaxed in a deep, alcohol induced slumber. "Thank God," he murmured.

She never even flinched as he lifted her out of the car and tucked her against his chest. Nick carried her into his place and laid her out in his bed, removing the cuffs and massaging the angry red marks that had arisen where she'd struggled against them. He tugged off her boots and socks, too, smiling as he held her tiny feet in his hands. Her toes were painted a pretty silvery color, so cute.

He tucked her under the covers and kissed her lightly on the forehead. "Pleasant dreams, Heather," he whispered.

Chapter Thirty

~ Mack ~

Mack woke up feeling as if an entire convoy of supply trucks had run over her. Twice. Her mouth was foul and dry; her tongue, thick and fuzzy. She looked around and had absolutely no idea where she was. It was a harsh reminder of exactly why she didn't go clubbing more often.

She breathed a sigh of relief when a brief self-inspection assured her she was still clothed, except for her boots and socks, which she located just inside the closed door. She sat up, waited for the room to stop spinning, and tried to reason it out.

It was definitely a bedroom. Not hers. Not one she recognized. The walls were a neutral shade of cream; mocha colored panel drapes, thankfully closed, hung over the two windows. A Shaker-style dresser sat against the wall, a matching night table by the bed.

The faint smell of a familiar aftershave hit her as her olfactory senses came back online. She turned her head into the pillow and sniffed, confirming her suspicions. *Nick.*

Mack fell back onto the bed and groaned. What the hell was she doing in Nick's bed? More importantly, where was he? Had her secret fantasies been realized and she'd missed it?

Disjointed flashes of memory assaulted her pounding head: going to the bar, dancing, being held against Nick' broad chest, getting arrested.... Her stomach clenched as she remembered some of the things she'd said to him.

She groaned, wondering what had happened to her neat, orderly life. When, exactly, had she lost control? *When Princess Dee arrived*, a voice in the back of her head answered.

Yes, Delilah was definitely a problem. She'd blown in and thrown Mack's disciplined life into a form of chaos. But Mack couldn't blame Dee for this. No, this was totally her own doing.

In fact, none of it was Dee's fault. Not really. Yes, Dee was a selfish, vindictive pain in the ass, but Mack was ultimately responsible for her own behavior. It was not Dee's actions, but Mack's *reactions*, that were the real issue. Allowing her stepsister to goad her into acting so out of character was on no one but herself.

Lesson learned. Too bad she hadn't figured that out before the charity gala, and definitely before she'd gone on a Cuervo-fueled bender.

She listened for a while as she waited for her stomach to settle. The house was quiet, no sound of movement. When she got the courage to sit up again, she spotted the handwritten note propped up on the nightstand along with two white pills, a glass of orange juice, and her phone.

Good morning, sleeping beauty. Take the pills and the juice, they'll help. Feel free to use the shower and anything else you need. I'll be back soon. Please don't leave. – N

Mack looked at his bold, male script and sighed. The urge to flee before he returned was strong, but she refrained. She'd made her bed, so to speak, and now it was time to lie in it (or in Nick's, as the case was).

She dutifully swallowed the pills and washed them down with the juice, which felt amazing against her throat. Then she picked up her phone, squinted through the blurriness, and fired off a text to Jay.

Mack: *Brutus.*

His response was immediate.

Jay: *Love you. You okay?*

Mack: *Feel like roadkill.*

Jay: *No surprise there. Let the good detective make it all better.*

Mack sighed. It was hard to be angry with Jay,

even when he did something foolish, like try to play Cupid. His heart was in the right place. They were definitely going to have words about this later, though, including a long discussion on personal boundaries.

Mack: *Seize?*

Jay*: Covered.*

Mack*: You are a prince among men.*

Jay*: I know.*

Swearing off tequila for the rest of her life, she went into the bathroom, pleased to find that the detective was a guy who valued cleanliness. Like the bedroom, the bathroom was done in neutrals and uncluttered, very much like her own.

She turned the shower on full blast, waiting for the water to warm, then stripped and stepped in directly under the spray. Almost immediately, the pain in her head began to recede under the powerful jets and a strange, tingly sensation took its place.

There was something surprisingly intimate about using a man's shower. Of being surrounded with his scent as the steam billowed around her. Of sliding the bar of deodorant soap over her skin, knowing he had done the same.

She closed her eyes, conjuring images of Nick, naked and wet in that very shower. A slow burn started deep in her core, helping to ease the discomfort of the morning along with the aspirin and the hot water. Her sensitive nipples pebbled as she ran her soapy hands over them, accompanied by an ache between her legs.

Dare she?

Biting her lip and feeling unnervingly needy, she gave into the sudden desire that gripped her. She stroked herself, letting the scene play out in her mind. The sensations built and crested quickly, far more quickly than in her own shower.

Feeling only slightly guilty, Mack shut off the water and dried off with one of the huge, fluffy towels he'd been kind enough to leave for her. After all, it wasn't the first time she'd fantasized about the handsome detective, though doing so in *his* shower had added fuel to the fire.

She made use of his SpeedStick and finger combed her hair into relative submission. She debated using his toothbrush, too, but decided that was too personal and ultimately opted for a washcloth smeared with some Crest instead.

Clean and relatively alert, Mack felt sufficiently recovered to face her rescuer. She lifted her clothes to her face and wrinkled her nose. *What the hell*, she thought, eyeing the clothes he'd left out, presumably for her. She'd slept in his bed, pleasured herself in his shower, and used his stuff. Why not wear his clothes, too?

She grabbed the dark grey police academy T and drawstring sweats and pulled them on, taking a moment to inhale and appreciate the freshly laundered scent. She made the bed, then figuring she'd stalled long enough, padded down to the living room. A neatly folded blanket and pillow sat on the couch, answering her early question of where Nick had spent the night. She added "gentleman" to the growing list of things she liked about him.

The man himself was nowhere to be found. A brief walk through the place confirmed that she was alone. She stopped in the kitchen, drawn by the scent of coffee, then settled in the living room to wait.

She didn't have to wait long. Soon Nick came in carrying two white plastic bags imprinted with the name of the local grocery store. He gave her a genuine (and relieved?) smile when he spotted her sitting there.

"I was afraid you wouldn't be here," he confessed. "I didn't want to leave, but I didn't have anything suitable for breakfast."

"You didn't have to do that," Mack said, stunned by his thoughtfulness. Her voice was still rough and husky-sounding, thanks to the copious amounts of tequila she'd consumed the night before.

"I wanted to. Feel up to eating something?"

Surprisingly, she did. The aspirin and hot shower had done wonders. And, except for a bit of lingering embarrassment, she felt strangely at home in his place. "Yes, but only if you let me help."

"Damn right you will," he said with a crooked smile that hit her somewhere right around her solar plexus.

Working side by side, they prepared a nice

breakfast: egg white omelets with green peppers and tomatoes, fresh fruit, whole-grain bread, Greek yogurt.

"Do you always eat like this, Detective?" Mack asked. The guy did take good care of his body, so he was obviously doing something right, but short of a chef, she'd never met a man who put that much effort into cooking, especially for himself. Even Jay, who was all about proper nutrition, limited the majority of his fuelings to pre-packaged, balanced meal supplements (except of course when she cooked).

"Truthfully, no. I know it's cliché, but I'm more of a coffee and donuts kind of guy." He chuckled at her raised eyebrow. "I make sure I work it off, though."

"Then why go to all this trouble?"

"I wanted to impress you," he admitted. "I know you're into healthy eating and all that. But I have to say, this is really good. I could get used to this."

Mack couldn't have stopped the butterflies fluttering in her stomach if she wanted to. But Kent's prank was still fresh in her mind. She searched for any sign on insincerity on Nick's part and found none. A tiny thrill went through her at the thought that he had gone to all this trouble for her with no ulterior motive.

She cleared her throat and toyed with her omelet. "Mission accomplished, Detective. I'm impressed. And grateful. Thanks. For everything."

"Call me Nick, please. When a woman spends the night in my bed, I think she's earned the right to call me by my first name, don't you?"

Mack felt the heat rise into her cheeks. "Yes… Nick."

His resulting smile sent those butterflies into a frenzy. She cleared her throat. "Just so you know, about last night… that's not typical behavior for me."

Nick nodded thoughtfully before he replied. "I didn't think it was. Can I ask you something?"

She figured he'd earned a few rights of his own. "Sure."

"Why would a smart, beautiful woman like you go out with a guy like Emerson anyway?"

Mack got up and took her plate to the sink, carefully considering her response. It wasn't that she didn't have an answer, but rather that she didn't like the ones she came up with when asking herself the same question. But, since this man had plucked her off the stage in the middle of an alcohol-fueled pole dance, she figured he was already clued in to the fact that she wasn't Ms. Perfect.

"Because he asked," she said finally.

Nick joined her at the sink, staring at her as if she'd grown three heads. "Seriously?"

She shrugged. Unable to meet his eyes, she sipped her coffee and stared down at her plate.

"Jesus," he breathed. "Are all the men in this

town fucking morons?"

She scoffed softly, but deep in her chest, her heart beat a little faster. That didn't stop the next words from crossing her lips. "The kind who prefer tall, svelte blondes." *Like Delilah.*

When he didn't say anything more, Mack chanced a glance upward to find Nick looking directly into her eyes. "You know what men see when they look at a woman like that?"

Yeah, she knew exactly what men saw when they looked at Delilah. Femininity. Desire. They experienced an immediate rise in testosterone and the urge to fall all over themselves to get her favor. But she said none of that, biting back the words and shaking her head.

"They see guaranteed sex and bragging rights. But you know what they see when they look at you?"

"A woman who can bench press three times their own weight?" she quipped, her mind and heart scrambling to re-build those crumbling shields around her heart.

"They see a woman who is so beautiful, so damn smexy, it scares the crap out of them."

"Smexy?" Shocked and certain she'd heard wrong, she latched onto that. "You think I'm smexy?"

"The perfect combination of smart and sexy? Yes," he confirmed. "And they also know you are not the kind of woman who is going to give them what they want without a whole lot of serious time and effort, so they go for the low-hanging fruit, like Delilah. But you know what?"

"What?" She held her breath.

"I'm all about the time and effort, Mack."

Chapter Thirty-One

~ *Mack* ~

Her heart stopped, then began to jackhammer furiously against the walls of her chest. Surely, he wasn't saying what she thought he was saying. She tilted her head and found him looking at her with a combination of heat and promise, a look that made her body tingle and her mind think crazy things. "You are?"

He continued to hold her gaze — one of the few who could — and nodded. "I am."

"What exactly does that mean?" she whispered. She needed him to be very clear. No misconceptions or misunderstandings this time, because as the last few days had proven, she wasn't particularly good at looking beyond what she wanted to see.

His mouth curved slowly into a crooked, sexy grin. He really needed to stop doing that. It threatened to destroy every wall she'd been trying so hard to rebuild.

"Little slow on the uptake this morning, are we? Fine. I'll spell it out for you. I like you, Mack, and I think you and I... well, I think we'd be really good together."

She blinked. "You do?"

"Yes. Having you in my bed — regrettably without me beside you — seeing you in my shirt, making breakfast with you... I like it. I want more. A whole lot more," he said, his voice lowering suggestively.

Mack sucked in a breath. Nick stepped closer, close enough to feel the heat radiating from his body. His large hands came to rest lightly on her hips, making her skin burn beneath them. "I'm even willing to give up donuts." His eyes sparkled. "Coffee's a deal breaker, though. I need my coffee."

A brief war raged within her as her desire rose quickly, flooding common sense and her ability to reason with need and want. The air sparked and popped and crackled between them, filled with possibility. She wanted this man, wanted him with a ferocity she wasn't used to feeling, and why shouldn't she have him?

You barely know him. Her rational mind gave one last feeble protest.

It caved immediately beneath the intensity of her passion. *I know enough.*

Mack slipped her arms up around his neck,

feeling the press of his arousal against her midsection. Another bolt of lust surged through her, overriding the last of her doubts. "Coffee's good. I drink coffee."

"Do you?"

"Yeah. Organic beans. Slow roasted."

He groaned. "You're killing me, woman."

Being held in his arms felt so good, pressing up against all that warm, solid male flesh. It had been a long time since she'd allowed herself to get physically close to someone besides Jay, and even then, there was no comparison. Hugging Jay was platonic. Affectionate. Friendly. Hugging Nick was nothing like that. Her endorphins spiked and her hormones went into overdrive, and yet she still felt a sense of peace and comfort washing over her — along with a need to get even closer. Mack laid her head against his chest, the throb between her legs matching the powerful thump-thump-thump beating steadily beneath her ear.

She didn't want to let go.

He pressed a light kiss on the top of her head. "Mmmm, I like smelling my soap on you."

She liked the fact that he liked smelling his soap on her. She wondered how he would feel if he knew what she'd done in his shower that morning. That needy ache in her core grew even stronger, wanting more.

"Don't you have to go to work today?" she asked, tilting her head upward and curling her fingers into his hair.

He shamelessly used the opportunity to move his lips down over her ear, along her jaw, to her neck. He kissed her gently, running his tongue over her birthmark and making her shiver. "No. I took the day off. I wanted to make sure you were okay."

"You did?" she breathed, her eyes all but rolling back in her head. When was the last time a man had taken time off from anything for her? When was the last time a man had kissed her like this?

"Yes. I'd like to spend the day with you, get to know you better. What about *Seize*?"

"Jay's got it covered."

"Hm." Nick hummed against her skin, sending more shivers up and down her spine. Really, really good shivers. "Got any ideas on what we should do?"

She pressed her body against his hard length. "A few."

Nick pulled away enough to rest his forehead against hers and exhaled. "I want you, Mack. So fucking bad I can taste it. But I'm willing to work for it. I'm willing to wait. Say no and this stops right here, right now. But if we go much farther, it's going to get harder…"

Her fingers tangled in his hair, grinding her body against one particularly stiff part of him. "I want it harder," she breathed. "As hard as you can make it."

He groaned again, cupping her behind and pulling against his erection. "Most women want the candlelight dinners and romance. Candy. Flowers. Five-date rules."

"I don't eat candy, and a gourmet breakfast you made yourself is infinitely preferable to some stuffy, overpriced restaurant. Five-date rules are for women who don't already know what they want."

"God*damn*, Mack. I've been dreaming of getting my hands on this ass since the first time I saw you. It's even better than I imagined. I want to see it naked. I want to grab onto your luscious hips with both hands and watch as I sink deep inside and make you come. You sure you're up for this?"

Mack caught her breath, shocked and highly aroused by his raw words. No one had ever spoken like that to her. There was only one truthful answer she could give him. "Yes."

She was in his arms a heartbeat later, being carried back into the bedroom and dropped onto the bed. "I have to warn you, Mack, it's been a long time for me, and this is going to be quick."

"Quick is good," she agreed, feeling a sense of urgency herself.

Before she finished speaking he was looming over her, tugging his shirt over her head. He drew in a sharp breath when her breasts were revealed.

"Damn," he murmured in awe. "You are so fucking perfect..." He was on his knees, cupping her breasts in his large hands. Kneading them just right – not gently, just firmly enough to border on pain. His thumbs skated over her nipples, bringing them to instant, hard peaks. "Jesus," he muttered again, and drew one eagerly into his mouth like a starving man.

"Last chance to say no here, Mack."

Mack grabbed his head and arched into him, crying out as he lavished attention on first one breast, then the other. By the time he was finished, she was panting as if she'd just run a 5K. "Not a chance," she said breathlessly.

"Off," he muttered against her skin as he kissed, her stomach and tugged at the sweats. "I want these off."

She lifted her hips without hesitation, and he yanked them down and over her feet. "You have the sexiest little feet," he said, kissing her arches, sucking each one of her toes. Mack never knew she had a direct nerve travelling from her toes to her center before, but there it was, definite proof right there. She threw her head back and groaned.

Nick kissed his way up her leg, tonguing her flesh and laving open-mouthed kisses as he went. He paused when he reached her molten core. "Damn, you're sweet. Like honey." A moment later he buried his face in her sex. She'd known it was coming, but nothing could have prepared her for the wholly possessive way he used his teeth and tongue and lips to give and take at the same time.

The man had some *serious* skills.

He growled something, a single word muffled against her folds as colored lights dotted her vision and earthquakes rocked her very core. She pulled his hair and cried his name as she fell apart. Before the last of the aftershocks faded away, she was vaguely aware of the telltale crinkling of a condom packet and then he was pushing into her. Still tingling, she felt the most wonderful stretching as he invaded her, filling her to capacity.

"Oh, Mack," he grunted with great effort. "You are the hottest fucking thing on earth when you come. I swear I'll make the next one last longer, I promise."

Next one?

He eased out and then pushed back in, deeper and farther than before. She was wet and slick, thanks to his expert preparation, easing the tight passage, her inner muscles gripping him, not wanting to release him for even a moment. Her powerful legs wrapped around his hips and pulled him in deeper even as her nails dug into his back.

"That's it," he crooned, "take me. Take all of me."

He pumped into her like a man possessed. She loved the fact that he didn't hold back, didn't try to handle her as if she would break. Mack begged him in breathy moans to go deeper, harder, faster, encouraging him by digging her nails into his firm ass.

As the tension coiled in her body, she felt him

swell inside of her. "Come again for me, baby," he rasped, his husky voice enough to send her over the edge. With a masculine grunt he pushed deep and stiffened. She felt him throb and pulse, the absence of wet heat assuring her that he'd been responsible. She was glad that at least one of them had been.

"Jesus, Mack," he moaned, rolling to the side and taking her with him. Hanging on, curling into his body felt like the most natural thing in the world.

"I knew it," he mumbled into her neck as he tucked her even closer.

"What did you know?" she whispered, her body as limp as a wet noodle, eyes closed with bliss.

"That you'd rock my world."

Certain she was dreaming, a gentle smile curved her lips as she closed her eyes and let herself bask in the afterglow.

Chapter Thirty-Two

~ *Mack* ~

"I give," she somehow managed with the last of her strength. Her entire body had been reduced to one quivering mass of gelatinous goo. Her sex throbbed with aftershocks powerful enough to have her twitching for long minutes after he'd made her shatter into thousands of tiny pieces of light… *again*. Letting herself go so wholly and completely felt wonderful.

"Music to my ears," he chuckled, pressing gentle kisses against her heated flesh. How he had the energy to do that was beyond her. She couldn't even summon the strength to open her eyes, and he'd been doing most of the work. The man had been like a machine, ringing every last possible drop of pleasure from her eager, willing body. After hours of lovemaking, sometimes tender and slow, sometimes hot and fierce, he finally seemed content.

"Are you always this... ardent?" she mused, wondering at the husky quality of her voice, most likely due to the screaming. And he had made her scream, which was really impressive, because she'd never had sex good enough to compel her to do so before.

"No," he admitted. "It's you. I can't get enough of you. I'm not sure I ever will."

She snorted softly. Even amidst the euphoria of post-coital bliss, she was afraid to believe that the "whole lot more" he'd mentioned earlier extended beyond their marathon sexy times. Doing so would just be opening herself up for all kinds of hurt. After the last twenty-four hours, she was pretty sure Nick Benning could be the one to *really* break her heart.

But only if *she* allowed it.

Instead, she began to rebuild those walls he'd already started breaking down — first with his gentlemanly charm, then with his very *un*gentlemanly ravishing. Those walls would have to remain in place for now, at least until she was convinced he wasn't just blowing smoke up her ass.

(To be fair, he really seemed to like her ass, and had spent a good portion of the last few hours letting her know that with words and touches that made all that glute work well worth it.)

"You don't have to keep saying stuff like that. I'm here, aren't I?"

His large hand flexed on her hip. "I meant

what I said, Mack."

  She curved her lips into a small smile. "You said you were all about the time and the effort. Well, you certainly gave me both."

 "Mack, look at me."

He coaxed her face toward his. Reluctantly, she opened her eyes and found him looking at her with concern. "What just happened?"

"Uh, we had great sex?"

His eyes flashed with heat. "After that. Just now."

She blinked, her gaze shifting slightly, away from his eyes and onto his forehead. She couldn't look into his eyes and tell him the truth, that she was falling hard and fast and was scared shitless. "I don't know what you're talking about."

"Detective, remember? And sweetheart, you're lying."

Deflection was also a valid option. "Is that your professional opinion?"

"*Mack*. Tell me what's going through that beautiful head of yours."

"Enough, Nick." She rolled away from him and planted her feet on the ground. Her legs felt like jelly. "Look, this was great. Really great, if I'm going to be completely honest. But you can stop with the hearts and flowers package. Clearly, it's not necessary to get me to sleep with you."

He recoiled as if she'd slapped him. "Seriously, Mack? Is that what you think? That I only said those things to get you into my bed?"

No, she didn't, and that was part of the problem. Buying into the image of happily ever after with him was too easy. But it — he — seemed too good to be true; therefore, he probably was. Only time would tell.

She shrugged. "You wouldn't be the first man to say things to get laid."

His expression grew darker, at once both tender and fierce. She wanted to get back into his bed, wrap her arms around him, and tell him the truth: that he had rocked her world too.

She didn't.

When he spoke, his voice was lower. Quieter. "Don't you feel it, too? This thing, whatever it is, between us? Tell me I'm not the only one here."

"You're not," she admitted carefully.

"Then what is it? Why is it so hard to accept that I want you for more than just your body, Mack?"

His words made her chest achy and tight. She wanted to believe him so badly, but past experiences and her recent humiliation had dug their claws in deep and refused to let go so easily. "I admit there is an undeniable attraction here, but don't you think we're getting a little ahead of ourselves?"

"No, I don't." Nick sat up, swinging his legs over the side of the bed so that he was facing away from her. He grabbed his jeans from the floor and stabbed his legs into them, then stood and turned. He hadn't bothered to fasten them. Her eyes were drawn to the trail of dark golden-brown hair that accentuated the lean cut of his hips and those two diagonal lines that short-circuited her ability to think rational thoughts.

"I've spent the last ten years of my life alone, certain that I would never again find someone who made me feel like this. And then I met you…" His voice brought her back out of fantasy land. He exhaled, running his hand over his face. "This was more than a quick fuck for me, Mack. I thought I was clear about that. I want more, and a few hours ago, I thought you did, too."

Yes, she did. The problem was, she didn't do anything by halves. She was either all in or all out, and she didn't have enough information to make that call. She couldn't go purely on her gut here. After hours of incredible sex, her judgment was skewed.

The warm glow in his beautiful eyes grew colder. She'd hurt him. Her heart ached, wanting to undo it, yet she couldn't. The words were right there, the ones that she knew would bring that light back into his eyes, but she just couldn't say them, because once she did, she was committed. The truth of it was, the intensity of her feelings for him terrified her. Despite her best efforts, she was falling hard and the ground below was coming up fast.

So she said the only honest thing she could. "I'm sorry, Nick."

His expression went neutral. He stalked out of the bedroom, leaving her alone. Her eyes filled with tears, tears that she would not spill, not there, not then. She blinked them away, focusing instead on pulling on her clothes from the night before. The smell of sweat and liquor was an unwelcomed contrast to the sweet, musky smell of their lovemaking.

Not lovemaking, sex, she corrected, sitting on the bed and slipping her feet into her boots, *no matter what it felt like*. Maybe she could try to talk to him. Tell him the truth. Explain her trepidation. Admit her fears.

Revealing your weakness will make it even easier for him to hurt you.

Mack heard him moving around in the kitchen, heard his deep voice muttering, but she couldn't make out what he was saying. Was he angry? Hurt? Or was he finally coming to the conclusion that she wasn't worth the time and effort after all?

Chapter Thirty-Three

~ *Nick* ~

Nick felt close to the edge. If he didn't remove himself from the situation, he was going to say or do something he'd regret and this — *she* — was too important to mess it up by pushing too hard.

He left her sitting on the bed, her eyes speaking volumes her mouth couldn't yet express. He got it, he really did. Opening her heart and soul to another was terrifying, especially when she'd been hurt in the past. He knew that better than anyone. But damn it, he wasn't asking her to walk down the aisle tomorrow.

Oh, he was convinced they were headed that way eventually, but they had a long way to go and a lot to learn about each other before then. For now, he just wanted her to take him at face value and trust him enough to acknowledge the possibilities. To embrace the potential of something *more*. Yet she seemed stubbornly determined to believe that this special connection between them was only a temporary thing. As if the idea that he wanted her for more than a cup of coffee and a friends-with-benefits type arrangement was inconceivable.

He'd thought he'd taken care of that by worshipping her with his body and his words, opening his heart, hoping she would see that it wasn't just about the sex. For a few glorious hours, he thought it had worked. Mack had been right there with him, accepting it all and giving everything right back.

He'd felt it deep in his soul.

Then the doubts started creeping in again, rearing their ugly heads and stealing the light from her beautiful eyes. The wrongness of it made him want to rage at everyone who had ever let her down.

He'd told her that he was all about the time and effort, and that was true. But at some point, Mack was going to have to take a leap of faith and trust that he would be there to catch her when she did. That he wouldn't simply walk away when he'd gotten what he wanted.

Like he just had.

Just like that, the light bulb went on as realization dawned: Mack was testing him.

She might not even realize she was doing it, but consciously or subconsciously, she was opening the door and giving him the opportunity to walk away. *Expecting* him to by giving him a push, making it easy.

Well, fuck that.

He turned around and stalked back to the bedroom to find her dressed and lacing up her boots. She looked up at him, her eyes holding a mix of resignation and hope, which she quickly hid away behind that implacable mask she gave the rest of the world.

"You're leaving?" he asked, crossing his arms over his chest and leaning against the door frame. Her eyes flicked over his chest and arms before drifting downward to the top of his unfastened jeans. Lust flared in her eyes. That was good. He could work with lust.

"Yeah." She exhaled. "I think I should."

He disagreed. He liked her right where she was and it was on the tip of his tongue to tell her so. However, if she was afraid to trust him, to trust her own heart, then words alone weren't going to cut it. Neither would giving in to his inner caveman and spending another couple hours making her scream with pleasure, however much he wanted to.

Oh, it was easy enough to get her to believe that he found her physically attractive and desirable enough to spend an entire afternoon hot and sweaty in the sheets. Not so easy to convince her he wanted the whole package, smart mouth, combat boots, and all.

And he *did* want it all.

Eventually, she'd come to realize he was a man

who meant what he said and said what he meant. For now, the ball was in her court, and he'd have to summon some of that patience he'd been talking about.

"All right," he nodded. "I'll give you a ride."

"I can call Jay," she offered.

And let her think that he didn't care enough to see her safely home himself? Not a chance.

"It's no problem. It's on the way to the station." He felt her eyes on his back as he slipped on a button down and grabbed his sport jacket, glad the station dress code was business casual.

"I thought you had the day off."

He gave her a small smile. "I do, but it looks like my plans fell through."

She bit her lip, an uncharacteristically vulnerable tell. "I'm sorry."

"Don't be." He leaned over and pressed a kiss to the top of her head. "Take all the time you need to wrap your head around this. I'm not going anywhere, Mack."

Nick dropped her off at her place. He got out of the car and walked her to the door ignoring her feeble protests that it wasn't necessary.

"Mack, I know it's not necessary, just as I know you are perfectly capable of taking care of yourself. Don't begrudge me for wanting to spend a few extra moments with you, okay?"

Something flashed in her eyes — approval, maybe? Hope? Didn't matter. It was another step in the right direction.

Nick cupped her face and leaned down, pouring the rest of the words he wanted to say into his kiss.

"I'll call you later, okay?"

"Okay."

Nick waited until she went into the house, then reluctantly walked back to his car and drove over to the station. Emerson nodded curtly in greeting, then went back to whatever he was working on. The guy was sporting a nice shiner. Nick didn't feel bad about that at all.

He'd barely sat down when the chief called him into his office. He exhaled, preparing for a lecture on decorum outside the office and how it reflected on the department. Instead, Chief Brown pointed to a seat and closed the door.

"You're going to want to hear this. I've got Special Agent Bartholomew on the line. Let me put him on speaker. Go on, Bartholomew. Benning's here."

"Detective Benning, glad you're there. I was just telling your chief the good news."

Nick looked questioningly at the chief. "What good news?"

"That information you provided has been instrumental in identifying the key players in the Necromancers. Some of those names weren't even on our radar, but thanks to you, they are now. Even more importantly, we've got a direct line to some possible suppliers on the east coast by connecting a few dots based on your legwork."

"Glad I could help."

"We'd like you to come down to our Philadelphia Division for a couple of days if possible. We're pulling together a task force, and we'd like you to be on it."

It was a great opportunity; one Nick would be a fool to pass up. He looked at his chief, who was nodding and beaming like a proud papa. "Yeah, sure. When?"

"We convene first thing tomorrow morning. I'll email you the details."

"No problem." Philly was only about two hours away by car. "And thanks."

"See you tomorrow, Detective."

Chief Brown disconnected the call, smiling broadly. "I knew hiring you was a good move. But do me a favor, will you? Next time you want to make a point with your fist, do it somewhere a bit more private, eh?"

Nick rubbed the back of his neck and grimaced. "Yeah, about that…"

The chief put up his hand to stop Nick from saying anymore. "I heard what happened, and off the record, he had it coming. I had to stop Gail from punching him herself when he came in this morning," he chuckled, then sobered. "Mack is a damn fine woman, and she sure as hell didn't deserve that. But I can't have my men brawling in public, got it?"

"Got it."

"Good. So… you and Mack, huh?"

Nick grinned. "I'm working on it."

"You have your work cut out for you."

"Nothing worthwhile is ever easy."

Sam laughed. "Ain't that the truth? Gail made me cross hell and high water, but getting a ring on that woman's finger was the best damn thing I ever did. Now, go bring Galligan up to date on your other cases and prepare for those suits in Philly tomorrow."

Chapter Thirty-Four

~ *Mack* ~

Nick: *Hey beautiful.*

Mack smiled down at her phone, Nick's latest text sending ribbons of warmth through her. She wanted to believe so badly, to trust that these feelings she had were real, because if they were, she had found her unicorn — a real, live, honest-to-God Mr. Right.

Mack: *Hey yourself.*

Nick: *How are you feeling?*

Lonely. Horny. Needy.

Mack: *Tired. A little sore.*

He answered with a winking smiley face.

Nick: *I have to drive down to Philly for a few days, but I'll have my cell with me. You know, in case you want to sext me or send nudes.*

Another GIF appeared on the screen, this one of a smiley face waggling its eyebrows. Mack laughed out loud as she tapped her reply.

Mack: *In your dreams, stud.*

Nick: *You're not wrong. Rest up, beautiful. I'll call you tomorrow.*

Mack: *Goodnight, Nick.*

Nick: *Goodnight, Heather.*

"What's got you grinning like a loon?" Jay asked, breezing into the room. "Wait, let me guess: Mr. Yummy Detective. I'm right, right?"

Mack couldn't deny it, nor did she want to. "Right."

"That man is all that and a bag of baked multi-grain chips — good for the body *and* the soul. So… I want details."

"Not a chance."

Jay pouted dramatically. "I share the details of my love life with you."

"No, you don't, nor do I want you to," she said on a laugh. "It's enough to know that Marcus makes you happy."

"And the yummy detective… does he make you happy?"

Mack sighed heavily. "Yes. But…"

"But…?"

"But… you know that old saying, 'if it seems too good to be true, it probably is'? Well, that's it in a nutshell. Nick Benning seems too good to be true. He's kind, smart, funny. A good listener, too."

Jay waved his hand dismissively. "So am I. That makes him good *friend* material. What about beyond that? Does he give you the tingles in all the right places?"

"Yes. God, yes."

"Then it's a no-brainer, baby girl. You have to give this a shot. Trust your instincts. Follow your heart."

There was a difference between knowing exactly what you wanted at that moment and what you wanted for tomorrow, next week, next month, next year. Sexy times with Nick? That was a no-brainer. An instant and resounding hell, yes.

But beyond that? Who could possibly make that kind of a decision after knowing someone casually for a few weeks? Sure, he seemed like the perfect man. Strong. Honorable. Kind. Intelligent. Funny. Not only willing to be with her, but actually *wanting* to.

"But what if he breaks it?"

"Then we'll break every part of him that matters," Jay said, an unusually somber edge to his voice. "But for what it's worth, I don't think he will. That man has it bad for you, Mack."

Does he, Mack wondered? Jay must have used his special BFF powers to read her thoughts because he said, "Yes, he does. Why is that so hard for you to believe?"

That was an excellent question, the answer to which was probably rooted deep in her psyche and decipherable only with a degree. "I don't know. Let's just say, life experience tends to suggest otherwise."

"Bullshit," Jay scoffed. "When are you seeing him again?"

"I don't know. He's going to be away for a couple days. Police business."

"Perfect! I'm calling Marcus."

Mack narrowed her gaze. Jay had a gleam in his eye, the same gleam he always got when he dreamed up some grand scheme. A ripple of foreboding went through her. "Why?"

"Because it's time to step out of your comfort zone and own that shit. Your man is not going to know what hit him when he comes back."

"Jay, we've tried this. The makeover? The Charity Ball? Ring any bells?"

"Yes, and for the record, you looked amazing."

"But it wasn't me."

"Exactly. That's where we went wrong. We're going to bring out your inner you. Unleash the sexy beast inside you."

"Jay…"

Jay stood, grabbed his phone, and held up his hand. "La-la-la, I can't hear Mack. Talk to the hand, baby girl, and just leave everything to us."

Four Days Later

"Looking good, Mack." Jay nodded approvingly at the high-definition screen.

"I can't thank you enough, Jay. All of you." She looked around at the half-dozen male models that had volunteered to help out. She hadn't realized how hard these guys worked. Who would have thought three hours in front of camera could be so exhausting?

"Anything for you, Mack," one of them winked.

As they headed for the locker rooms, Mack felt gratitude and a sense of pride. The gratitude came from their unselfish willingness to do a pro-bono shoot. The pride, a result of professional appreciation for their beautifully-sculpted bodies, bodies which she had helped hone to optimal fitness.

They were good guys, guys she'd known since Jay brought them to *Seize* when she first opened. They'd been offering to help her ramp up her advertising with some free publicity, but she'd felt weird about using them that way. Jay, however, had no such reservations, and had set up a campaign with his partners in collusion, Marcus and Tish. The idea was to promote *Seize*, Tish's agency, and the male models. A win-win-win.

"I don't know about this, Jay," she said, biting her lip as she looked at the digital proofs from the shoot. She had to admit, she looked *good*. Of course, a French bulldog would look good in the middle of those guys.

"I know. That's why I'm not giving you a

choice. I've already sent them to Tish."

"You did that in the two seconds it took me to grab some water and thank those guys?"

"Welcome to high speed internet, Mack," he quipped, flashing her a grin. "Didn't want to take the chance that you'd chicken out." He glanced down at his phone. "And FYI — Tish has already approved the release. She loves it! Says you're very photogenic."

Mack snorted.

"Seriously. Strong is the new skinny, and honey, whether you know it or not, you are an inspiration."

Mack focused on the inspiration part as she wiped some of the body oil from her chest and arms. If she could inspire just one woman to feel empowered, then it was worth it. After all, that was what *Seize* was all about — giving people the means to take control of their own lives and create their own success stories.

"And when Mr. Yummy Detective sees that…well, I give it thirty minutes, an hour tops, before he's tossing you over his shoulder and taking you back to his man cave."

A thrill ran through her. Mack wasn't exactly the submissive type, but a show of primal male posturing from Nick could be all kinds of hot. He was on a very short list of people she'd be willing to give up control to for a little while.

"Not gonna happen. He's in Philly all week."

She knew, because she was counting the hours until the weekend when she would see him again. They'd been talking on the phone every night while he was away, and he'd been texting on and off throughout the days. She missed him, more than she would have believed possible after knowing him for such a short time. Her body craved him, too. Apparently, those sexy times they'd shared had broken the seal, so to speak, and now she found herself wanting more. A lot more.

She was starting to believe Jay was right. Maybe she should stop overthinking things and follow her heart.

"You sure about that?" Jay smirked. "Because I'm thinking he might head back early *if* he had the proper incentive."

Mack closed her eyes and exhaled. "You didn't. Jay, tell me you didn't."

"Didn't what? Snap a few pics and send them to his phone?"

"Jay…"

"Ah, speak of the devil and he doth appear."

Mack's heart sped up when she whipped around and saw Nick standing in the doorway.

"Jesus, Mack. The way he's looking at you… *I'm* getting hot."

Chapter Thirty-Five

~ *Nick* ~

"Hey."

"Hey." His voice was rough, strained. Getting even that one word out was an effort. It was all he could do not to march right over there, toss her over his shoulder, and spend the next hour in the nearest convenient utility closet.

She was so fucking hot, and incredibly, she had no idea. He could see it in her eyes.

When Jay had sent him those pictures, pictures of her among all those guys, he'd nearly gone out of his mind. Lust, jealousy, pride, want … they all surged and rallied. Thankfully, the task force had just been finishing up. He'd all but run to his hotel, packed his shit, and hit the road, the need to see her a powerful, tangible thing.

The Fates seemed to be on board with his plan. With minimal traffic and inactive construction zones, he made the trip back in record time. All the way, he'd been warring with himself. On the one side, his more primitive side, he couldn't get to her fast enough. The other, more civilized side warned about doing anything that might push her away and cautioned restraint.

He said he'd give her time to wrap her mind around things, and he would. Even if it killed him. Which it just might.

Looking at her now, those two opposing factions continued to battle. Torn between the need to gather her into his arms and his desire to give her the space he'd promised, he remained rooted to the spot, hands tucked into his pockets to avoid reaching out to her.

The room emptied out. Jay was the last to leave, laying a hand on his shoulder as he passed. "Go get her, tiger."

"You're back early." Mack remained where she was at the center of the room. Too goddamn far away.

"We wrapped things up quicker than expected."

She smiled, a slow, seductive grin that tugged at his hardening cock. In his mind, he heard the sound of her coming, an echoing loop of the phone sex they'd engaged in the night before. He was willing to wait, but he wasn't stupid. He was going to use every advantage he could to bring her around, including the explosive sexual chemistry between them.

"Yeah?"

He swallowed hard. "Yeah."

She began walking toward him. No, not walking, stalking. Putting all those luscious, toned, oiled curves into motion. "Does that mean you're free tonight?"

"It does."

"Huh." She stopped right in front of him. Close enough for him to feel her heat. Scent her unique feminine fragrance — a mix of fresh citrus and essential oils that he would forever associate with her. He inhaled deeply, drawing her into his lungs. The pupils of her lovely green-gray eyes dilated, letting him know she was right there with him. *Thank God for that.*

"Got something in mind?" he asked.

"I have a few ideas." She leaned in close until her lips hovered just below his. "I missed you."

"I missed you, too."

"Talk is cheap, Detective. Show me."

He couldn't have stopped himself if he tried. Between one heartbeat and the next, the small space between them vanished and his arms were pulling her in tight against his body. Their lips met in a fierce kiss. Teeth scraped, tongues danced, and the rest of the world faded away until it was just the two of them.

He didn't know how much time passed before he registered the catcalls and insistent knocking on the window behind him. Reluctantly, he softened the kiss, then pulled away far enough to say, "I think we have an audience."

Her eyes opened slowly, looking every bit as hungry and passion-drunk as he felt. "You're place or mine?"

"Which is closer?"

"Mine," she answered. She grabbed his hand and led him through the corridors to the entrance like a woman on a mission. "Anxious?" he teased.

"You have no idea."

"Oh, I think I have a pretty good idea."

Minutes later, they were pulling up to Mack's place. Mack jumped out and practically ran to the door. He was right on her heels. As soon as Mack punched in the security code, they were tumbling through the door like horny teenagers.

"Did I ever tell you how fucking sexy you are in camo?" he managed, using his bigger mass to back her against the door. "Take it off. Now."

She bit his lip, her hands already making fast work of his pants. She lifted her arms, allowing him to tug off her super sexy sports bra crop top thing. He wasted no time in dropping his head and sucking one of her lovely breasts into his mouth, mumbling claims against her skin.

She tasted delicious. And so very *his*.

Mack moved like lightning, circling his arms with her own, and sweeping with her legs as she twisted, taking him down onto the floor.

"Your woman?" she said, straddling his chest.

"Is that what you just said?"

A tensing of muscle was the only warning he gave her before he thrust upward with his powerful hips and grabbed her arm, rolling her smoothly beneath him. "Yes. Got a problem with that?"

Instead of fighting, she used her weight and rolled with the momentum, coming up on top again. "That depends."

He clenched his jaw, heat firing in his groin as she rocked over him and teased him with her beautiful breasts so close to his mouth. "On what?"

"On whether you're man enough to handle me or not."

"Oh, I'm man enough." He rocked his stiff cock against her. Desire flared in her eyes. "And I want nothing more, *Heather*."

She stilled at the use of her first name; he held his breath. His hands flexed on her hips. Either she would accept his claim or she wouldn't.

She stared down at him, the corner of her mouth twitching. "Giving up already?"

He gazed up at her, eyes blazing with hunger. "Are you kidding? Why would I fight this? I've got you exactly where I want you now." He looked hungrily at her crotch and licked his lips even as his big hands managed to palm her ass, just in case she had any misguided notions of moving.

She glared at him, then her lips twitched. "You do, huh?"

"Yeah. Except..."

She raised a brow.

"Except you're supposed to be naked and about two feet higher, straddling my face."

"You're an idiot."

"Yes, but I'm your idiot."

"You sure about that?"

Nick braced his legs and lifted his upper body, causing Mack to slide down onto his lap. He caught her with his arms and brought his mouth crashing down hard on hers. He pushed his tongue into her mouth and laid exclusive claim.

When he finally pulled away, he stared into her dazed eyes. "Yeah," he said huskily. "Damn sure."

Mack responded by tangling her fingers in his hair and gripping hard.

Minutes later, they were both naked and he was poised at her entrance. "Say it, Mack. Say you're willing to give us a chance."

She looked at him with those beautiful eyes so filled with desire and something more. "Yes, Nick, I'm willing to give us a chance. But if you—"

He didn't give her a chance to finish whatever she was going to say, pushing deep inside her and making her moan in pleasure. She grinned, her inner muscles flexing around him, making him see stars as she started moving, riding him as if her life depended on it.

Then she was screaming his name, and all was right with his world.

Chapter Thirty-Six

~ *Mack* ~

"I don't know what the hell we were thinking," Mack muttered to herself, looking over her hefty to-do list. Hosting a Thanksgiving dinner for nearly a dozen people? It was right up there on the list of brilliant ideas with fostering a K9 recruit who hadn't quite made the cut. Clearly, Nick's repeated and arduous attentions had addled her brain. He'd learned quickly that when he gave her that crooked smile, her resistance (and good sense) melted.

The cunning devil came up behind her and slid his arms around her waist, his four-legged partner in crime at his heels. "Thanksgiving is all about family, Mack. Yours. Mine. *Ours*."

Mack didn't feel the sense of panic those words would have brought on only a few months earlier. Every day she fell more in love with the man, and no longer wasted energy on worrying about what *might* happen. They just *fit*, two halves to an even better whole. Mack wasn't the type to get overly sappy or romantic, but she *was* incredibly happy.

"Yes, but…"

He bowed his head and nibbled at the sensitive area just below her ear, laying waste to her defenses. "No buts. Except this one, right here."

He pressed his hardness into her backside, a gentle, rhythmic thrust that had her ready to abandon her list and spend the rest of the day in bed with him instead.

"Are you two at it again?" Jay teased, coming into the kitchen with Marcus.

"Says the man who hasn't kept his hands to himself all morning," Marcus quipped, leaning over to give Mack a kiss on the cheek. He held out a baking dish, then searched for a spot on the already-loaded countertop. "You've got enough food here to feed an army. Just how many are you expecting?"

"My dad and his wife, Catherine, are flying out from the west coast," she told them, "and Nick flew his parents up from Florida. Plus Nick's sister, Liz, and her husband, Miles, and stepson, Brandon."

"No Delilah?"

"No. We invited her, but she said she had other plans."

"Yeah, neither of us is too broken up over that," Nick said, planting one more kiss on her temple then taking advantage of her momentary loss of focus by stealing two fluffy vegan biscuits (her own special recipe) — one for him and one for Kato.

The Shepherd-Labrador mix, who'd been on kitchen Hoover duty, caught the biscuit and offered a doggie smile. The 'five second rule' had become obsolete since he'd come along.

"What other plans?" Jay asked, frowning slightly. "She's not spending Thanksgiving alone, is she?"

"She didn't say and I didn't ask." Mack did wonder, though. Maybe Dee was still upset with her mother for booting her out of the nest. Or maybe she was still pissed at Mack for tossing her out on her ass. Regardless, that was one less thing Mack had to worry about. Where Dee went, drama was always sure to follow, and meeting Nick's parents had Mack nervous enough.

Nick kept telling her she had nothing to worry about, that they would love her. She hoped that was true.

If they were half as nice as his sister, things should go well. Mack and Nick had had dinner with Liz and Miles several times and Mack liked them very much. At first she'd been afraid she wouldn't, conjuring images of stuffy, very proper types after Nick told her proudly that Liz was a big deal in a local software engineering company and that Miles had been a successful, international businessman. She needn't have worried. They were nothing like her preconceived notions. Intelligent and well-traveled, yes, but also very down to earth, unpretentious, good people.

In just a few weeks, Liz was turning out to be more of sister than Dee ever was. Liz had even invited Mack to a "girls' night out" with her and her friend, Holly, which turned out to be a lot of fun. Holly wrote romance novels for a living, wasn't shy about discussing her 'research', and dropped the f-bomb almost as often as Mack. When Liz told Holly about *Seize*, both women joined up, so Mack got to see them several times a week. The pair were a riot and never failed to make her laugh and brighten her day.

On the other hand, she didn't worry about Nick meeting her dad, not at all. They were going to get along just fine. Both were strong men with solid foundations and a love for the outdoors (and, Nick told her, a shared love for *her*). As for Catherine, well, Mack didn't really care what she thought.

The doorbell rang and Nick grinned excitedly. "They're here!" He noticed Mack's momentary panic and said, "Relax, Mack. They're going to love you, just as I do. And word of warning: my mother *will* want to help." Nick turned to Jay. "Keep her from bolting, will you? Sit on her if you have to."

Jay laughed. "He's a keeper, baby girl."

As if she didn't already know that.

The murmur of voices and excited, happy greetings drifted into the kitchen. Mack smoothed her apron and tried to look casual and welcoming, but nothing could completely stop the flurry of butterflies that had suddenly taken up residence in her stomach.

"Relax," Jay said softly, draping his arm around her and giving her shoulders a squeeze. "Nick's right. They're going to love you."

As if sensing her unease, Kato came over and sat down at her feet, leaning against her leg. She reached down and petted him, the action calming her almost immediately.

A few minutes later, Nick re-entered with his sister and an older couple. The man was tall and broad, an older version of Nick; the woman was much shorter, with snowy white hair and the same kind, laughing eyes as Nick.

"Mom, Dad, this is Mack — Heather MacKenzie. Mack, my parents, Ed and Lynnette Benning."

Mack found her voice. "Mr. and Mrs. Benning, it's wonderful to meet you. I'm so glad you could make it."

Nick's mom beamed. "It's nice to meet you too, Mack. Thank you for having us."

"It smells amazing in here, Mack," Liz said, following in behind them with Miles and Brandon. "What can we do to help? And don't even think about saying 'nothing'. Making Thanksgiving dinner together is half the fun."

"She's right," Lynnette said, pushing up her sleeves. "I haven't had a chance to prepare a proper holiday feast in years."

"In that case, I would love some help."

Nick winked over his mother's head and grinned. "Told you," he mouthed.

Mack got them both aprons and put Nick's mom in charge of the dressing, then handed Liz a colander of washed vegetables and pointed her towards a machine that cut, sliced, diced, and spiraled. "Create something beautiful."

Liz beamed in approval. "I'm on it. Hey, Nick, the Shelby's running a little rough. Would you mind taking a look?"

Nick's eyes lit up. "Yeah, sure. You good in here?"

"Yeah, we're good," Mack waved him off. "Go bond."

"Mind if we tag along?" Marcus asked.

"Not at all. What do you say, Dad? You want to see the Shelby and check out the 1970 SS396 Chevelle I picked up while we're at it?"

Ed Benning, who had been looking a little lost, brightened. "The Shelby?"

Liz laughed as the men filed out, talking excitedly about Nick's latest acquisition. "Some things never change. Nick has always been obsessed with classic muscle cars, and Brandon is just like him."

Mack's father was the last to arrive. George MacKenzie pulled her into a big bear hug, lifting her off the ground.

"Isn't Catherine with you?"

A frown ghosted over his features. "She sends her apologies. Delilah called earlier and asked to see her."

"I invited Delilah," Mack told him.

"I know you did, sweetheart. Now where is this young man I keep hearing so much about?"

Her father's deliberate change of topic signaled the end of the conversation as far as Catherine and Delilah were concerned. Something was going on there, Mack was certain of it, but she wasn't going to let that cast a shadow on the day.

"He's out back, showing the guys his new toy. I'll take you out and introduce you."

"No need, I can introduce myself," George said gruffly, leaning down to give her a kiss. "I just need to know one thing: is he treating my baby right?"

Mack grinned. "Yeah, he is, Dad."

George nodded. "Then we'll get along just fine."

"Your dad is a lot like mine," Liz said on a laugh.

"A good man never stops caring for his daughter, and you will always be your daddy's little girl," Lynnette agreed.

With Liz and Lynnette's help, the dinner came together beautifully. It was a lovely combination of traditional family recipes and healthy, vegan options. The atmosphere around the dinner table was friendly, lively, and at times, loud. Mack soaked it all in, embracing the spirit of the day by being thankful that they had all come together.

Nick suddenly cleared his throat and stood, raising his glass. "Thank you, everyone, for coming today. To family, both new and old."

Everyone raised their glasses and murmured their agreement.

"And while we're all gathered here, there's something else I'd like to say." He paused, ensuring he had everyone's attention, including Mack's.

"I never thought I'd find true happiness again, but Mack has changed all that. I've fallen deeply and madly in love with her, and I'd like this Thanksgiving to be the first of many, many more to come, if she'll have me."

Mack gasped as Nick kneeled down beside her and took her hand in his. "Heather MacKenzie, will you marry me?"

"Short and to the point. I like that," Mack's father said, making everyone chuckle.

Mack looked into Nick's eyes, seeing her future. A future of love, of life, and of laughter. There was only one answer.

"Yes."

Nick smiled and whistled softly. Kato came padding up and dropped a small box into Nick's hand. "My wingman," Nick said.

Nick took out the ring, a simple, stunning solitaire, and slid it on to Mack's finger to the applause of their friends and families. Mack cupped his face and kissed him solidly. "You sure about this?" She whispered softly.

"Baby, I've never been surer of anything in my life."

Epilogue

~ *Mack* ~

One year later...

Mack looked over the top of her tablet at her new husband, still somewhat shocked by the last quarter's numbers. There was actually a waiting list for full memberships, and Booty Camp classes were booked for the next six months.

Nick was finishing off the last of the organic, gluten-free pizza — a new recipe Mack was considering for her latest nutritional guide — and holding the crust just out of reach of Kato. The lack of focus that had kept the big brute from being a professional drug sniffer didn't seem to be an issue now. The dog's concentration was absolute.

Kato was now a permanent part of their family. Nick insisted that adopting the goofy (but incredibly cuddly) furbaby would give him peace of mind for those times when he was working late, but Mack knew better. Nick had an even bigger, softer heart than she did. She'd known from the moment Nick first brought Kato through the door that he'd found his forever home.

"You have to give it to him now," she said, waving her hand at the dog. Each time Nick moved his hand, Kato's eyes followed as though hypnotized. "Look, he's sporting a total ear boner."

Nick paused and shot her a disbelieving look. "Ear boner?"

"Yeah," she nodded pointing to the way Kato's ears pointed toward the ceiling. "See how they're sticking right up like that? That's called an ear boner."

"You're making that up."

"Am not."

"That is *not* a real thing."

"Of course, it is. Google it."

He thumbed his iPhone, doing just that. "Son of a bitch."

"Doubter," she smirked. "Go on, give him the crust at least. There is another pie in the oven for you."

Nick tossed Kato the crust and stood. "Shit!" he exclaimed, slipping on his first step forward.

"It's your own fault. If you hadn't teased him like that, he wouldn't have drooled so much."

"Seriously?"

"Yeah. It's like black ice. You don't see it until

it's too late." She reached over and grabbed a towel off the counter and tossed it to him. Nick grumbled a little as he dropped the rag on the floor and wiped with his foot, but Mack caught the discreet scratch behind the ear that he gave the dog.

"Speaking of hidden pitfalls, have you heard from your stepsister lately?"

"Yeah, she's still pissed that I didn't send her a housewarming gift."

"She tell you that?"

"Sort of. She sent me this." Mack held up her phone to show him the series of symbols that comprised Delilah's latest text: (_*_)

"What is that?"

She grinned. "The emoticon for an asshole."

Proving that karma was alive and well in the world, Dee and Kent Emerson had moved in together. *The Playboy and the Princess*. No one had seen that one coming, but no one was complaining, either. With Dee and Kent focused on each other, everyone else could breathe a sigh of relief.

"Yep. She's pissed." Nick pulled her into his arms and kissed her long and hard. "Your dad cut her off, for real this time?"

"Yep. He said since she's living with Kent, she's his problem now, and Catherine actually backed him up. After Dee's juvenile stunt last year, I think Catherine's finally seen the light."

"You mean when Dee called her mother feigning some crisis to keep Catherine from having

Thanksgiving dinner with us?"

"Uh-huh. Dad told me that Catherine genuinely regretted not coming, especially when he told her how much fun we all had without her." Mack grinned. "Though it probably worked out for the best. Catherine has a gift for making people uncomfortable."

"Well, all I can say is, Kent and Delilah deserve each other," he said.

"That they do," she agreed. "But you know what? I hope they both find happiness. As long as it's not anywhere around us."

"What about you?"

"What about me?" she asked.

"Are you happy, Mrs. Benning?"

Mack crawled up her new husband's body, wrapping her arms around his neck and her legs around his waist. "Deliriously."

"Yeah?"

"Oh, yeah. You?"

"Yeah."

"Christ, you're bare," he muttered running his hands along her strong, shapely thighs. He held her with one arm, using the other to push down his sweats and free himself. Mack wasn't the only one who went commando around the house. It proved convenient for when the urge to make love to his beautiful wife surged, whenever and wherever they were.

She nipped his bottom lip and stroked his hard

shaft with her sex, doing some kind of body rolling motion she picked up in one of those stripper classes. "'Cause I think I could make you happier…"

Nick laughed as he shifted her onto the counter and slid home. "I doubt it. But I'd sure as hell like to see you try…"

Thanks for reading Nick and Mack's story

Would you like to read a special exclusive bonus scene?

Sign up for my newsletter today! You'll not only get advance notice of new releases, sales, giveaways, contests, fun facts, and other great things each month, you'll also get a free book just for signing up *and* be automatically entered for a chance to win a gift card every month, simply for reading it! Plus access to subscriber-only exclusive bonus content.

Get started today! Go to **abbiezandersromance.com** and click on the **Subscribe** tab to sign up!

Also by Abbie Zanders

Contemporary Romance – Covendale Series

If you like humor and snark in your romance, add a stop in Covendale

- 📖 Five Minute Man
- 📖 All Night Woman
- 📖 Seizing Mack

Contemporary Romance – Sanctuary Series

Small town romance and romantic suspense featuring former military heroes.

- 📖 Protecting Sam
- 📖 Best Laid Plans
- 📖 Shadow of Doubt

More Contemporary Romance

- 📖 The Realist
- 📖 Celestial Desire
- 📖 Letting Go
- 📖 SEAL Out of Water (Silver SEALs)
- 📖 Rock Star Romeo (Cocky Hero Club)

Cerasino Family Novellas

Short, sweet romance to put a smile on your face

- 📖 Just For Me
- 📖 Just For Him

Time Travel Romance

Travel between present day NYC and 15ᵗʰ century Scotland in these stand-alone but related titles

- 📖 Maiden in Manhattan
- 📖 Raising Hell in the Highlands

(also available as a box set)

Paranormal Romance – Mythic Series

Welcome to Mythic, an idyllic communities all kinds of Extraordinaries call home.

- 📖 Faerie Godmother
- 📖 Fallen Angel
- 📖 The Oracle at Mythic
- 📖 Wolf Out of Water

More Paranormal Romance

- Vampire, Unaware
- Black Wolfe's Mate
- Going Nowhere
- The Jewel
- Close Encounters of the Sexy Kind
- Rock Hard
- Immortal Dreams
- Rehabbing the Beast
- More than Mortal

Howls Romance

Classic romance with a furry twist

- Falling for the Werewolf
- A Very Beary Christmas

Historical/Medieval Romance

- A Warrior's Heart (written as Avelyn McCrae)

About the Author

Abbie Zanders loves to read and write romance in all forms; she is quite obsessive, really. Her ultimate fantasy is to spend all of her free time doing both, preferably in a secluded mountain cabin overlooking a pristine lake, though a private beach on a lush tropical island works, too. Sharing her work with others of similar mind is a dream come true. She promises her readers two things: no cliffhangers, and there will always be a happy ending. Beyond that, you never know…

Made in the USA
Coppell, TX
15 June 2022